VERANDAH
PEOPLE

VERANDAH
PEOPLE

stories by

JONATHAN BENNETT

RAINCOAST BOOKS

Vancouver

Raincoast Books acknowledges the ongoing financial support of the Government
of Canada through The Canada Council for the Arts and the Book Publishing
Industry Development Program (BPIDP); and the Government of British
Columbia through the BC Arts Council.

Edited by Lynn Henry
Typesetting by Teresa Bubela

National Library of Canada Cataloguing in Publication Data

Bennett, Jonathan, 1970 –
  Verandah people / Jonathan Bennett.

  ISBN 1-55192-649-0

  I. Title.
PS8553.E534V47 2003   C813'.6   C2003-910386-2
PR9199.4.B46V47 2003

Library of Congress Control Number: 2003092552

Raincoast Books   *In the United States:*
9050 Shaughnessy Street   Publishers Group West
Vancouver, British Columbia   1700 Fourth Street
Canada   V6P 6E5 Berkeley, California
www.raincoast.com   94710

At Raincoast Books we are committed to protecting the environment and to
the responsible use of natural resources. We are acting on this commitment by
working with suppliers and printers to phase out our use of paper produced
from ancient forests. This book is one step towards that goal. It is printed on 100%
ancient-forest-free paper (100% post-consumer recycled), processed chlorine- and
acid-free. It is printed with vegetable-based inks. For further information, visit
our website at www.raincoast.com. We are working with Markets Initiative
(www.oldgrowthfree.com) on this project.

Printed in Canada by Friesens

10 9 8 7 6 5 4 3 2 1

For Wendy

CONTENTS

"Verandahs are no-man's-land, border zones that keep contact with the house and its activities on one face but are open on the other to the street, the night and all the vast, unknown areas beyond."
— David Malouf, *12 Edmonstone Street*

VERANDAH
PEOPLE

Boys drink, hidden behind trees, when they are underage; until they are no longer underage but young men with apprenticeships; until they are no longer young men with wages in the pocket of their dusty shorts but young fathers with children and a wife to feed and provide for; until they are no longer young but among the dead in a prisoner-of-war camp in a country their mates cannot spell or find on a map, or are made unexpectedly unmarried once again either by cancer, or a drunk driver, or their swinging fists letting loose on her thankless grin after a long week at work and thirteen glasses of beer; until they are no longer young but middle-aged and sad, or poignant, or frightened; until they are no longer working men, but pensioners, diggers, grandfathers, old men who tell of the times when things were different all the while knowing they have not changed in any measurable way at all.

MARCUS LISTENED TO THE RAIN keeping an imprecise rhythm as it fell sharply on the corrugated iron roof. Tonight, his wife's absence was so heavy and certain as to almost stir in the bed next to him. He felt stillness where her shallow breathing used to touch the skin of his neck and saw nothing where her brown-grey hair once splayed across the pillow in a fan. On their last night in this bed together, months ago now, he had thought Judith's breathing sounded uncomfortable. She had twitched every now and then, disturbing him, her dreams keeping him awake. But tonight he was left with only the rain. Its unorchestrated pings on the roof.

The next morning, dry-mouthed and with an unsteady hand, he tea-spooned instant coffee crystals into a mug. How could they possibly cure him, he thought, such tiny things. Judith's alarm clock had rung minutes after he'd finally drifted off to sleep. In a rage he'd torn the plug from the wall. The clock face had cracked as it struck the doorframe.

Filling the kettle over the sink, Marcus's eyelids ached if he forced them to remain open and stung when he allowed them to close. He'd slept like an awkward-limbed teenager, an uncoordinated sleep that performed self-consciously before the edge of the day. Right before the alarm sounded, a single, fractured dream had begun. It made use of the only noise around him — the rain — to create a scene with Judith in the shower, her soapy legs, clouds of steam, and the smooth, familiar strokes of her razor running the length of her shin bone and calf muscles. The alarm woke him up before the blood, before any horror could develop.

The kettle whistled. Marcus considered the twenty minutes that remained before he was due at a job — the big place at the end of the point. The old woman, who'd phoned yesterday quite out of the blue, had asked for a quote on some exterior work: painting a detailed verandah, some stripping, varnishing and a whitewash. Is it still raining? he wondered. Can't exactly paint outside in bad weather. Marcus stopped and listened, wondering if he was up to it, if or why he should be bothered at all. The roof was silent.

The kettle stopped whistling and he poured a cup of coffee that tasted bitter. There was nothing to eat in his fridge and so he eyed the cereal box on the table. It was his young son, Kevin's, and had been left out since the boy's last visit — a week ago now. This reminded him: he must pick Kevin up from school today. It was Dad's turn again. Would he ever get used to this, only having his boy for twenty-four hours every seven days? Did she know what she'd done to him, and to his little boy, to *them all*? He had never been unfaithful; he had always worked hard, fed them. Marcus put his hand in the cereal box and crunched on a few sickeningly sweet Froot Loops then drank more of his coffee. He felt like Judith's greasy eggs and sausages. He felt like shit.

A LOW MASS OF LEAD-COLOURED cloud hung over the bay, a mist of rain pressing down on the still water. As though it were robbed of oxygen, the strip of bush separating sky from water shed only a faint hue, a blue with red sympathies, almost periwinkle. Gum trees could, in a certain light, appear blue. They were blue now. Not as blue as ink, but a light silvery blue. This was the scene upon which Marcus turned his back as he stepped in through the open door of the house beside the bay, at the end of the point. He regarded the painting on the wall opposite him.

He stood before it like a witness, as if it were the accused. It showed a partial doorframe, and through the doorway there were chairs under an overhanging verandah that led out to grass and garden — a sun-filled day outside, depicted from the inside. He admired the prominent dabs of colour in this typical scene: blues, greens, yellows, and oranges.

"You're here for the verandah?"

Marcus turned toward the old woman's voice.

"Yes," he said, noticing she had a touch of England still left in her accent. "My name is Marcus Page." His eyes ran over her thin arms, her slender fingers.

"Please include all your expenses, Mr. Page. I don't want anything to be charged extra at the end." She led Marcus through the old house and out to the verandah. "My name is Mavis. This house is called Forby's Rest." Once outside, it was clear to Marcus the scene all around him inspired the painting he'd just viewed. The verandah ran along the four sides of the house; the overgrown garden and grass looked as if it loved this rain.

Marcus dug a nail into the wet base of the verandah's railing. With a few twists he gouged down through the years, through the coats of paint to the wood. He wasn't sure what type it was. He pushed the nail in again. A good, hard wood, though. Knew that much. The woman, Mavis, wanted green trim, white railings, varnished floorboards. Alone, the work would take him two weeks. Mavis had a blue Jaguar in the driveway. He'd ask for two thousand. Why not? If he didn't get the job, he'd go down the coast fishing with his cousin. What else did he have to do now?

Marcus looked out at the bay through the lightening drizzle. He thought about Judith, how she had long dreamed of being free of him. She'd wanted him to do the leaving, him to deal the blow. She'd wished he would fall in love with some other woman. In her twitching dreams, he knew she pretended that if she were free, without her husband, she would be different altogether. She would pursue romance with foreigners, with men like the Americans and Englishmen she watched on TV, she would move into a terrace-house in the city, walk her golden retriever, eat sashimi, mix drinks with Cinzano and fresh lemon, she would drive a restored MGB.

He knew she imagined these lives as her eyes wandered during their dinner conversations to an imaginary horizon, as the distance between them at night widened. For years she bet on time and on her strength. He could do nothing to please her. He watched her private plot develop and harden: during birthday-cake wishes, horoscope predictions, and exotic holiday novels. She negotiated him out of her plans. Her plans. It's out of my hands, he thought. My hands. He fingered the nail. *Your bloody hands are all you've got.*

He wrote out the details of the quote on his stationery. At the bottom he totalled the bloated numbers. Then he scrawled: "Please call within forty-eight hours if you want me to start the work before the weekend. Thank you, Marcus Page." He stuck his quote to the front door, got into his truck, and drove to The Workers Club for lunch.

As he bit into his hamburger, egg yolk and beetroot juice leaked onto his hand and ran down his hairy forearm. Marcus licked the gold and burgundy stream before taking a gulp of his beer. The Club's doors were wide open to the hot day so the salty outside air bled into the thick smoke and stale beer fumes. A horse race started on the television. Marcus thought he recognised the two young men at the table next to him. The two sat close together drinking Bundy and Cokes, and chain smoking. They were talking so loudly he was forced to eavesdrop. Their conversation circled about a surfing accident, winter waves, and girls.

Marcus ate a chip drenched in barbecue sauce then glanced outside across the street. Against the sheer white wall leaned a woman: short red dress, legs, long hair. Marcus bit through his tongue. Judith! He tasted blood as he swallowed his chip. But this woman, this version, was too young. Marcus became faint at the taste of himself. She was too tall. He tossed back his beer in a single long swig. Besides, Judith was renting a small flat more than half an hour's drive away. She was not here at all. Not until tomorrow. And now one of the boys recognised the young woman.

"Mate, she puts out, they reckon," said one to the other.

Marcus got up to leave as the other patrons cheered on the televised horses thundering down the backstretch, TAB tickets in hand, drunk, noisy, mates and strangers, all Australians together, sharing that peculiar kind of egalitarian male love, bound, loyal and cheerfully trapped in a gorgeous oblivion.

MARCUS PARKED HIS WHITE TRUCK across the road from his son's school. He was early. He should take Kevin straight home today, he thought, as a black dog strolled down the sidewalk and stopped beside his truck. Marcus and the dog looked at each other for a few seconds before the dog continued on its way. A dog, thought Marcus. I could get Kevin a puppy. Something for him to take away. He'd like that. Marcus turned the key and threw the truck into gear.

Through the wire mesh, animals of every description either curled into furballs in the corners of their cages, or sprang at Marcus as he walked past, ignoring the fence that separated them. The only real choice was from a litter of German shepherd mongrels. But none of the puppies looked into his eyes the way the black dog had at the school. Still, with luck, a dog, any dog, would remind Kevin of his father. Somehow he could have a place in his son's new life, Judith's new life. He pointed out a German shepherd pup to the attendant. The runt.

As Marcus pulled up to the school in his truck, he saw Kevin standing on the curb holding his teacher's hand. Marcus could see that Kevin's eyes were red and reckoned the boy had been crying.

"We thought you'd forgotten him," said the teacher, Mrs. Underwood, giving Marcus a look up and down that made him think of the beer that had accompanied his hamburger.

"I saw your father-in-law, down at The Workers Club, drinking," said Marcus. She didn't respond to this diversion. Marcus took Kevin's hand, thanked Mrs. Underwood for waiting, and helped Kevin up into the truck.

The German shepherd pup lay shivering on the middle of the seat, wrapped in a blanket.

"Look what I got for you, mate."

Kevin's thin legs dangled in the air off the seat, searching for Marcus's toolbox to rest on. The boy stared out the window, facing away from his father and the puppy, looking back at his kindergarten teacher across the road.

"That's why I was held up, Kevin. It's for you."

Marcus followed his boy's gaze. He saw the teacher, her one arm bent with her hand up on her cheek, the other arm moving slightly, either waving goodbye as an afterthought or unconsciously beckoning. Marcus put his key in the ignition. Kevin reached out and put his forehead on the window-pane, his small head quivering with the truck's vibrations. Although his gaze remained fixed out the window, Marcus watched Kevin's fingers creep across the seat to the pup. Then his grubby little hand stroked the dog in slight, reassuring movements.

When Kevin had first arrived, his tiny newborn hand had stretched out and gripped the face of Marcus's diver's watch as if it were a discus. *And now it's a little man sitting there,* thought Marcus, *staring out the window, pissed off at his dad.*

On the way back home, Marcus stopped the truck near a clifftop overlooking the sea. It was a spot he'd taken Kevin to several times before. Marcus thought of it as their spot. Where had this morning's rain disappeared to? Marcus hung his elbow out the truck window. He smoked, looking at Kevin, at his little short legs — Judith had once said his little legs were like string and sticks — resting up on his toolbox.

His son stared down at the ocean rising and sinking in heaving oscillations the size of whole tanker ships. There was a southerly wind passing through the open truck windows when Kevin finally spoke to him. Marcus did not answer, his mind distracted, thinking of Judith, Judith in bed, Judith showering, of his meeting tomorrow morning with Judith — the forcible surrendering of it all. For it *was* the beginning of the end. This much he'd begun to understand. His Friday nights and Saturday mornings with his son would, eventually, be taken from him too. Nothing was fair or honest anymore; he would lose what little he had left. With only one hand he could snap her neck.

THE NEXT DAY, KEVIN RAN across the restaurant's huge verandah, between the white plastic tables and chairs, the umbrellas, the American tourists, the wealthy locals, yelling *Mummy*. Before Marcus had even had a chance to tighten his grip on his son's hand, Kevin had spotted her and was off, elbows, heels, sticks, string. Marcus watched him run and anticipated his path, his eyes overtaking his son, darting between waiters and patio furniture, hats and menus, sunglasses and silverware, before finally resting on Judith.

Marcus saw her arms outstretch, anticipating her five-year-old son's pain. She'd had a haircut. She'd bought that green dress last Christmas as a present to herself. *To Judith, love Judith.*

She kissed her son on the forehead. "Me too, me too, darling," she was saying as Marcus approached, as he took a seat opposite, as he adjusted his chair, as he looked up at her face, as he looked back down at his hands lighting a cigarette.

The waiter suddenly stood over Marcus, his head performing an eclipse of the sun. Marcus looked to Judith.

"Just for coffee, I think," said Judith.

Marcus said nothing; he'd forgotten his lines.

"Two coffees, thanks," Judith said.

He saw and remembered her white teeth. Her green dress, white teeth.

"Mummy missed you."

She was speaking to Kevin now, almost ignoring Marcus. Her words floated about in the air, and his mind grasped to hold onto them, onto her voice, the sound of it. It all seemed too thin somehow. Too complicated. He looked at his hands and thought of the verandah work. It had to be done this week. Whitewash. Green trim.

"It's okay, Kevin, you can tell Mummy. What's in the car, sweetie?" she said.

In the painting he'd seen at Mavis's, the thing missing, the part that should have been included, was a person. Maybe two people. Such a sunny day and such a colourful garden. Why did the artist stay inside but paint the outside? A verandah is outside. But it's a shelter, kind of half in, half out. So it wasn't a painting of the garden, it was a painting of the verandah — a bit of the bedroom and a bit of the garden had been needed in order to show it being a thing whose essence was both inside and out. Brilliant, he thought. But, regardless, there should have been people in the painting.

"Marcus! Why does Kevin have a puppy? You know I only have

a small flat, until the settlement. I told you that — unless you'd care to speed things up." He thought her beautiful, and shrill, and found himself grinning a little.

"Dad, Mummy's crying. Mummy, why are you crying?"

"Mummy is not crying, honey. It's just that Mummy wishes your Daddy would think about someone other than your Daddy."

Then she grabbed hold of herself, turned to the business of why they were meeting. Judith talked a stream of words lost to him: lawyers, and restrictions, and payments. He had nothing. Nothing to contribute to her demands and declarations, and soon a lawyer would find out that he also had nothing left in the bank to give her. Forby's Rest was the first job he'd done in months. He'd spent their savings in fits and spurts, on drink, on the horses. Even though he'd been the one who had earned most of it in the first place, when they found this out she'd get the house, its tin roof. He knew how these things worked.

Marcus watched Judith leave with Kevin dragging behind, his arm pinned in the air, only half completing his steps, drifting a little, like an astronaut. Marcus's eyes followed them as they wove their way through the umbrellas and menus, the silverware and waiters, through the smoke of his cigarette and the bitterness of his coffee. He turned and looked the other way.

The restaurant overlooked the sea: blue, hard, and flat like a postcard. Yesterday's swell had died right down. No good for fishing or surfing, he thought. This pretty sea was only for looking at. It's what the American tourists at the next table were busy doing, sipping their breakfast vodkas, rounding their Rrrrrs. He glanced back for a final look, scanned the crowd for her green dress. His floating son. They'd gone.

Marcus wandered through the park on the way back to his truck. He kicked off his thongs and felt the tough grass gouge his feet. The park ran across a gentle hill. Norfolk pines planted as windbreaks and sand traps stood in rows. Marcus's eyes rested on a lone Moreton Bay fig, its thick, webbed roots like toes spread out into the sandy soil. Marcus lay down not far from it. He ignored the great trunk and roots etched with lovers' initials, tattooed with local rock-band names, scarred with xenophobic slogans.

As he lay there on the rough grass he felt something pressing down on his chest. It was dense, loud, and tall. It was out of focus and he couldn't see past it. He found it so hard to breathe that his eyes filled with tears, his mouth watered and ached, his stomach turned over once before he could fight off the nausea.

What're waves, Dad?

Yesterday, in the car, Kevin had looked over the cliff down at the heaving sea. The dog's chin had been resting on Kevin's stick and string legs. *How do waves bounce?* the boy had asked. He'd patted and stroked the puppy. It was scared but it had licked Kevin's knee with a flash of pink tongue.

When Kevin had asked him about waves, Marcus had been thinking of Judith. Of her breath at night, of her weight in the bed, of how, right until the very end, she had still touched him even though she dreamed of others. Was it just habit? Was their life together merely the ballast against which she offset her hopes? He'd had nothing to tell his boy about the waves.

The sun was high in the sky. Despite the coffee and his racing heart, Marcus dozed. He'd had so little sleep of late. The final blow would come soon. He felt nothing, other than tired. He slept.

An hour later, Marcus made his way back to his truck. He opened the front door, releasing oven-like air. The puppy lay on its side, its pink tongue slack, its eyes sunken. It had died of suffocation. Or perhaps thirst. Or heat exhaustion. He'd left his truck unlocked, but the windows were rolled up. He assumed Judith had taken the puppy with her hours ago, that Kevin would have insisted. Marcus reached in and picked up the tiny dog, held it in his palm. It was warm and had a loose weight about it. Marcus put the dog in an old plastic bag that he found under the seat of his truck and tied a knot in the top. He walked it over to a rubbish bin in the park.

"WHAT TIME OF A MORNING do you begin, Mr. Page?"

"Oh, Mrs. Crawshaw. Seven-thirty, usually." Marcus smiled at Mavis. He realised how he knew her. Years ago she'd been on the shire council. Besides, this house, Forby's Rest, was well-known locally. From the water, when he'd been fishing on the bay, he'd often looked up at it standing there on the point. Its great gold and red sandstone blocks muscling into the trees, and leaded glass reflecting the light, sky and water.

"You work more like an artist than a painter, Mr. Page."

"My dad was a painter. I went to art classes in Sydney after high school."

"Oh, goodness. I was commenting on your speed rather than your talent. Now I've hurt your feelings." Her grey hair resembled steel wool.

"Not at all. I didn't finish art school. Anyway, I charge by the job, not the hour."

"Cup of tea?"

Marcus rested on the verandah, his legs dangling free off the edge, and waited for his tea. The extraordinary garden unfolded before him down the gentle slope.

"Mr. Page, could you help me here, please?" Her voice came from around the side of the house. Marcus followed a path through the garden and found the old lady with a hammer in her hand trying to remove a nail from the trunk of a huge gum. "Who put this here!" she said. Marcus obliged. He took the hammer from her hands and pried the nail free. "It's a terrible thing," she said as he handed her the offending nail. Marcus followed her inside for tea.

"I'm getting old now, Mr. Page. The years have compressed together. I wake up in the morning and it's Christmas. Then it seems the next morning when I wake up, again, it's Christmas. But you're an artist, you know this already. What do you like to paint?"

"I don't paint anymore. But that picture in your foyer, of the verandah. Who painted it?"

"Well, I finished it, but I had help from a friend who sketched it and started it. But this friend, her name is my little secret."

"So it's from here, this house?"

"Yes, it's the view from the guest bedroom at the front, through the verandah out to the garden. Do you like it?"

"I do."

"Grace would be pleased. Oh, there, I said her name. Never mind. This house is full of paintings. My father was an artist and he had many like-minded friends. Forby's Rest was an enchanted place to be a young girl."

Marcus painted white railings until the shadows from the trees made it difficult to see where his second coat needed touch-ups. The rest of the family had all trickled home by late afternoon. Marcus heard them eating together in the garden, Mavis doing most of the running back and forth to the kitchen. He left by the side path so as not to disturb their meal. He stopped when he noticed the sap. It was leaking in a fit of protest from the hole where he'd pulled the nail from the tree — a geyser of ruby molasses. His stomach was now calling for food and beer.

THE NIGHT SWIRLED BEFORE HIM. During his dinner of beer and chips, a woman who had once been his babysitter had approached him. She chatted him up. This woman was living back at home, at her mother's place until Christmas. And was he married? And how old was his son? She left smiling, saying, see you later. Then his cousin had arrived with a few mates and they all bet on the dogs in Brisbane. Marcus lost $170. He ran out of smokes — borrowed money from his cousin. Bourbons. A joint in the parking lot. Then that woman, the babysitter, again. In the cab of his truck he struggled to work his jeans far enough down his thighs. She remained almost clothed, only throwing a leg over. He guessed at what she was like through her T-shirt. They touched each other's skin only where necessary.

Driving home in his truck he caught sight of his toolbox on the floor. The little stick and string legs. His little man. Should go and kick that teacher in the guts, know-it-all bitch. The dark road out into the National Park was straight and driving along it at night with the reflectors to guide you wasn't hard, it wasn't hard to steer if you were a bit pissed, a bit bloody pissed. Right, eh, Judith? Got a problem with m' drinking. I got a problem with your bloody not drinking. I gotta piss like a racehorse.

Marcus pulled over. Cock in hand, he drew wet lines up and down a tree trunk and destroyed a nearby ants' colony. Force majeur.

In the bush the shapes of the trees at night and the noises made him laugh: stupid bloody trees, he shouted, bloody bitch, ya bitch. Where was the truck, or the road? His left sandal became twisted and he fell, cracked his head on a rock, collapsing no more than one hundred metres from his truck.

MARCUS OPENED HIS EYES the next morning to a bright day. The sun warmed the skin on his neck. His hand felt out the extent of the dried blood caked across his face, following it upstream, back to the cut on his head. He saw his truck, staggered to it, and grabbed his red toolbox. *Can't be late for Mavis.* Her old face smiled at him, her grey hair, her thin fingers reaching for his cheek to pat it gently.

By crashing through bush and hoisting himself over rock faces, Marcus climbed a hill. From the top he could see the horizon, the hazy line where blue sky meets blue sea. The top of the hill was flat and sparse. His eyes fixed on one specific tree. A tall gum tree with scribbly bark. The handwriting of tiny insects whose tracks and trails wound and twisted tangled, innate journeys.

It means something, he reasoned, wildly, crying aloud: "I can read a scribbly gum, Mavis. Come, come here." Then, after a time, softer, "Come, why don't you."

This lone tree was distinct from the surrounding bush — a tattooed arm. Marcus lugged his toolbox over to the tree. His fingers copied the patterns, followed the tracks of the insects, chasing their earlier wanderings. From the toolbox he got out his hammer and a long nail.

TWO AMERICAN BUSH WALKERS found him the next day on the hilltop. They were themselves lost and had climbed the hill for bearings. The unframed picture they witnessed was a body slumped at the foot of a scribbly bark tree, his arm raised. From a distance he seemed to be waving, or beckoning. A red toolbox lay at his side.

The sweet smell of the blood that raced down his hairy forearm from where it was attached to the tree had attracted a black feral dog and her litter of puppies from a sandstone wind cave not far away. The old girl had approached first. She licked at the blood, at the flesh of his arm and at the sap that was already hardening into rivulets of translucent red glass. She bit at his leg, then yelped for her pups to join her.

When the two Americans stormed onto the scene waving and shouting, the dogs with their twelve little mouths full of new nipping teeth fled, having left only punctures. The first man ripped Marcus's hand off the tree. It was the other one who carried Marcus, like a sack, for three hundred metres until they heard cars.

GROPING
HEAD

THE DAY BEFORE SHE DIED, Aunt Mavis fussed about the kitchen looking to be helpful. Opening the refrigerator she'd found a bag of green beans. With the bag dangling from her mouth, she took her dull paring knife from the drawer and went out onto the verandah. Sitting in her rocking chair, Mavis methodically topped and tailed each bean.

As she worked, a kookaburra swooped down and landed on the lawn. Did their eyes meet; were thoughts exchanged? She returned to the kitchen and picked a sausage from the fridge. On the verandah she broke the skin and threw pieces of the raw minced meat to the kookaburra. The bird snapped up each bit and thumped the meat on the ground as if to kill it, swallowed in a succession of jerky movements, and finally flew off over the house, likely landing in one of the trees at the other end of the garden.

Groping Head is a place too small for all but the most obscure, local maps. It nods out into the Pacific Ocean off the east coast of Australia. To say more would be to add prosaic directions. You'd be hard pressed to find it anyway. It's enough to know that my family home, Forby's Rest, sits at the base of the headland. It's the last house on Nullaburra Parade — the one with long, yellow-white sandstone blocks and a bottle-green verandah that runs around all four sides, the big house that is all but enveloped in garden. It's colonial in shape, but has an odd Mediterranean feel to it that is hard to put your finger on.

My aunt, Mavis Crawshaw, woke every morning to the sun climbing its way over Forby's Rest and down the six ghost gums.

"These old gum trees that run along the house's west side," Mavis would tell a first-time visitor, "I left 'em standing for years as a shield from the wind and sun. Those branches up there — they're tangled up now. Didn't used to be that way."

Forby's Rest still enjoys local fame for its garden, Aunt Mavis's garden. Each day she'd pull weeds and check plants for lace bug or caterpillars. This past year she was surprised to find that she had tomatoes.

"Who planted them?" For days she muttered this.

But her garden employed its own logic. It wove its own twill of fruit and vegetables that grew around and in between shrubs and flowers; native flora and fauna competed against exotic English cousins for water and light. Because the garden was fashioned mostly by sheer chance, plants would die here and there; some of the fruit would taste sour.

Many people offered her instruction, tips, solid rules of green thumb, and Aunt Mavis often listened, always smiled. But she knew her relationship with each plant, and it was not based on economics or aesthetics. For Mavis, her garden was about how high a shrub stood and of whose shape it reminded her; or which child hid under what tree; or how a leaf touched the fingers. "There must always be moss!" she would occasionally say.

No, and thank you, Mavis liked her garden growing just how it was meant to — linked branches reaching and playing out like lost summer conversations, single leaves breathing, turning, scattering — eventually decaying.

Groping Head borders a national park. My grandfather,

Percy Southworth, was a barrister, but he also painted landscapes. His motivation in moving here was to capture, in paint, Groping Head's cliffs, bush, and sea. You can tell by his renderings of wind, sunlit rock, and dense low brush that the land induced vigour in this Englishman living in self-imposed exile.

The painting that still hangs in Mavis's bedroom is his. It's of Little Wobbygong Beach in 1924. In the middle distance two female figures in navy striped neck-to-knees are wading at the shore. The sea is pale blue, the windblown breakers are white, the sand is afternoon gold, and the cliffs in the distance reflect the pinks and oranges of the setting sun. The dark-haired woman is my grandmother, and the child holding her hand is my Aunt Mavis. It is the only known Percy Southworth painting that depicts people.

"I like it on my wall, it soothes me," Mavis would explain, as she wrapped up the tour for new visitors. "When I am writing in my diary I look up at the painting, at that beach, and it brings all the outside in. And at the same time it lets me, when I'm trapped inside, get out to it."

I'd been watching her feeding the kookaburra that day from the kitchen window. After the bird ate and flew off, she got down on her knees and pulled weeds. Then, as always, she wrote in a thin book. After a cup of tea, she went back out and sat on the verandah. Finally, I gathered my thoughts and went out to speak with her.

"Deakin," she said when she saw me. "I was pulling weeds out and I've realized that some of it is parsley. Imagine that." I followed her out into the garden, as I had done my whole life, and down the overgrown path. She reached for a bunch of bright green that she'd picked earlier and left by a sapling. "See." She chewed a sprig of parsley for a moment. I took a piece from her hand; the folds of her skin were marked with thin lines of dark earth.

"Aunt Mavis," I began to ask. "Do you still want me to walk with you to Little Wobbygong Beach today, for a picnic?"

She looked through me for a moment and then walked away, as if she'd suddenly forgotten to do something important. I followed several steps behind. When she got to the verandah and started to write in her book I decided to give up waiting for an answer. She was old now and often forgot trains of thought, or where it was she'd been off to.

It was the very next day, some time during her afternoon nap, with the lazy sunlight warming her face — because the leaves on the ghost gums outside her window now have too few leaves to provide decent protection — that we generally suspect my Aunt Mavis took her final breath. This last act of the living matters less to me now. Death is subjective on Groping Head.

"I THINK CAPTAIN COOK discovered Australia on this very sand," she once said to me as a boy. Aunt Mavis told me many enormous fibs when I was a child. "He'd have anchored on a flat day and rowed in. He and Banks would have stood right here. A day or two at least before they ever found Botany Bay." And she marked an X in the sand with her big toe. We were on Little Wobbygong Beach. I was only ten, but I remember her hair wild in the winter wind, as clearly as if my memory was a painting.

She also talked about the weather a lot. That day she'd said, "It's a sou'easter, Deakin, right from the south pole." We'd made our way up the beach, sitting on the coarse grass. It was almost summer, but it was very cool that day and she wore a navy cardigan, a white long-sleeved skivvy turned down once at the neck and tucked into her gardening pants, and she carried a book.

When she began to write, I grew bored and ran down to the water's edge. I remember a sailboat inching up the coast, towards Botany Bay or further perhaps, to Sydney Heads, on a wide, wide reach. At my feet an eyeless fish lolled about with each small wave's ebb and flow, rotting, its white flesh hanging off it in strands, helpless, swollen, dead.

"Tea, Deakin?" she called.

I ran up the sand and fell down beside her on the tartan rug she'd spread out. She produced a silver thermos from her basket — the smell of Earl Grey quickly lost to the wind. The hot, sweet tea worked hard in my mouth against the salt and seaweed in the air. She offered me the choice of an Arrowroot biscuit or a blood plum. I ate both at once.

"Deakin, your father has asked me to be the one to tell you this. Last night, your mother died in the hospital." The biscuit turned to paste in my mouth, as it dried out and I gasped at the air for breath. This was why we were here at the beach having fun. This was why we were not at visiting hours.

After that first utterance she'd made, I don't remember exactly what Mavis said — her words seemed to clot, soft and bloody dark with hard centres, as if they were seeds. I played with the felt tassels on the blanket, staring into the Black Watch pattern of it. Then I was seized with panic, unable to look up for fear of losing concentration. It was as if, to me as a little boy, Mavis's words had become all there was of my mother. I'd felt that if I were to let these sentences slip away there might be no further mention of her, nothing left to hold Mum together in my mind.

Of my mother's funeral, all I recall is the prickly orange shirt Aunt Mavis made me wear, and all the other mourners in dark clothes, and for the first time, adults talking to me alone, in unfamiliar tones. They discussed my mother, as if I knew her cooking secrets, her traits, her perfume, her habits, as if I were a man.

It was perhaps because of this sudden thrust into adulthood that I retreated into the relative safety of boyhood for the rest of that eleventh summer of mine. The smooth, slow days of December and January that swell up and out of my past are not associated with sorrow for me. They are not dark or sad, but light and thrilling. There sits Aunt Mavis at the kitchen table, yesterday's *Sydney Morning Herald* outspread to catch rinds and pips as she spoons out purple passionfruit flesh, and twists navel oranges to mix her "juice of the sun."

Back then, she had hair the same colour as local grey mudstone, and she'd say: "Go back outside and dry off before you come in this house." So I'd tear out into the morning warmth, run and jump back into the sea, salt stinging at my eyes, the water swallowing me whole as I slowed down and floated up to breathe. Whatever grief I'd felt at the loss of my mother was dissipated by what life seemed to offer me as a boy. I'd never felt so alive.

Those summer months we swam, attempted to bowl googlies, ate mangoes right off Aunt Mavis's tree in the garden, and had swirling hose fights in the pre-sun hours. They were mornings

GROPING HEAD ■ 35

of swimming and cricket washed in pink dawn light, before breakfast and the glasses of sticky juice, when only Aunt Mavis might know under which tree we played. I longed for that summer of boyhood to last forever.

Aunt Mavis and I would always wake first, even before the screeching flocks of galahs and cockatoos that still, today, live high up in the branches of the ghost gums. Then my mate, Dermott, would arrive on his bike at six with the sun. Sometimes we caught cicadas (green-grocers mostly, but also black-princes) and put them in glass jars to keep for bait, or pets. Aunt Mavis would say, "Tell Dermott to go home for breakfast, his mother won't know where he is." Then she would make Dermott and me toast and Vegemite to tide us over, until my father woke up and wanted juice.

"Give this bouquet to your mother for her table, Dermott." Aunt Mavis made arrangements out of native flora from her garden: gumnuts, bottlebrushes, and kangaroo's tails — back when you could pick them. Dermott's mother worked long nightshifts down with the fishmongers. Aunt Mavis had a soft spot for her, as her husband was never about. Mavis fed Dermott most of his meals. Dermott would often arrive with trays of fish and crab as thanks delivered from his mother.

"Dermott, you always bring the best seafood," Mavis would say with a smile. "You're lucky to have such a good mother."

It was only when the police caught Dermott's father that we all learned why he was never at home. Aunt Mavis, her spoon gouging out a passionfruit, read the newspaper through mounting citrus seeds and pulp: "Police in New Guinea uncover drug import ring and laundering. Fugitive caught." It was him alright. He'd been in Port Moresby on his way to Java. The police soon sent Dermott to Gracehurst Boys' Home. He was back within a month, but school had started once more, and our friendship was never to totally recover. We remained neighbours but became men in our different ways; he with a lost father, me a lost mother. For some, absences like these might have been the stuff from which lifelong bonds are made, but for Dermott and me they were only reminders of how life can turn away from you, how once a time has passed, it can never be again.

My own father was a quiet man. My mother's illness and death turned him so inward that he rarely spoke. He became all but a shadow in my youth, there, but inactive, not wholly unloving or uncaring, but inattentive. My mother's departure ruptured something within him. It was his sister, my Aunt Mavis, who therefore stepped forward — by design or circumstance I still do not know — to play the major role at Forby's Rest.

Belinda came into my life with two young boys. In the years that followed we married and together had a daughter. All three children knew Mavis differently than I ever did at their age. Grandmotherly, Mavis had only ever been very old to them. When the boys first arrived they'd play with the limp velvet flesh under her arms and chin. It would jiggle away and the two of them would laugh, and then laugh at their own laughter. She was so helpful to have around for their early years at Forby's Rest. They would play in the garden, hide, run, and hose each other, swim, and tan — just as I'd done. Aunt Mavis watched over them, as she had me, with one eye on the garden and the other on the boys. Writing in her book, when the moments turned slow.

When we all first lived at Forby's Rest — Belinda and her two boys, Mavis, my father, and myself — we would eat long dinners together and drink wine in the garden until well after dark. And when Dad died, Aunt Mavis stayed on with us. Or we with her. She, helping with our newborn daughter, writing, keeping the garden alive; Belinda and myself, working, continuing all that I had ever been a part of and known: the Southworths at Forby's Rest on Groping Head.

At my father's wake Aunt Mavis greeted each mourner: "Oh, hi, come on through to the garden, love." They'd follow her through the kitchen where lamingtons, crustless open-faced Vegemite sandwich trays, paper cups for the boxed white wine in the fridge, a plate of chocolate Tim Tams, and empty beer tins covered the draining boards.

Then they would say, "Mavis, should I have brought something …"

"Oh, love," she'd say. "It's barely a wake. Late lunch really. Your father hated a fuss, didn't he, Deakin."

Mavis had devoted her life to her brother, Forby's Rest, and to her extended family. Forby's Rest was all she knew. She loved to tell the story of how it came by its name: how my grandfather, Percy Southworth, the barrister, landscape painter and builder, spread his own father's ashes — his name was Forby Southworth — over the foundations. And so it is not surprising that when my father died on Groping Head, Mavis had felt he was precisely where he should have been. That his deteriorating health went unnoticed, and illness undiagnosed until it was much too late, was due partly to her overly loyal sense of duty to this house and land.

"Deaths are important to Groping Head," she remarked at my father's funeral.

IT WAS ALWAYS MAVIS'S WISH to be buried on the top of the headland. Everyone who knew her well was aware of this. It took three days of strings being pulled before an official in Sydney turned a blind eye and signed a letter that declared ten square feet on the top of Groping Head a private cemetery and an historical landmark, because of the "important contribution the Southworth family has made to the community." The funeral was scheduled for Sunday morning. The mourners were to walk from Forby's Rest, up the track, to the site.

So, because of these legalities, it was not until Saturday afternoon that I and several other locals — among them Dermott — came forward to lift the coffin up the half-kilometre bush track to the crown of Groping Head. Once there, we started to dig. We chipped away at rock and tree roots for hours. If it hadn't been for Mavis lying in the coffin right there, we might have given up shy of the required six feet. It was dark when we covered the coffin in a plastic tarpaulin weighted down with rocks on all four corners, and returned to Forby's Rest, exhausted, for beers.

I woke at five the next morning, dressed, and walked up the track for one last moment with her. First I saw the discarded tarp, and then the coffin itself ten metres from where we'd left it. Its lid lay wide open. On the lip of the coffin a kookaburra perched — something was alive in its beak. The bird thumped it against the polished wood. I clapped my hands as I approached and it took to the sky.

The morning air was cool and it brushed over my skin. Heart thumping, I immediately inspected the site, picking up rock chips as if they were clues, checking behind trees, anything to delay looking inside the coffin. What was going to be in there: the tracks or scratch marks of a feral animal, broken glass left by hooligans, unthinkable clumps of her hair, clothes, tracks of blood?

From the top of Groping Head I could see far into the distance. A sailboat flying an orange and black spinnaker caught my eye. Out of hopelessness, madness, I threw a rock at it, following the rock's downward arc. Seconds rolled by. The sailboat had to be beyond the natural horizon line. My sorry rock fell into the ocean below, lost into the swell. The coffin was empty. Mavis was gone. I panicked.

Running back down the track, my mind was wild with plots and red herrings. In the garage I got the wheelbarrow, hurried around to Mavis's bedroom window, climbed inside, loaded five heavy boxes of her books — in which she'd written her entire life — into the wheelbarrow, and set off back up the hill. On the crown I packed the books into the coffin, recovered it with the tarp, and placed rocks on all four corners.

When I finally fell into bed with Belinda it was six-thirty. I slept for another two hours. When I woke for the second time that morning it was to the sound of our daughter's voice: "Dad. There's still some of Mavis's 'juice of the sun' left. Want a glass?" The funeral went as planned. The coffin was lowered into the rocky grave. Collectively, we filled in the hole. Only I knew of the books we buried.

That afternoon in the garden I stood amongst Aunt Mavis's plants, her garden, her world, nodding to both friends and people I barely knew, listening to them tell me stories I'd heard before. By the time the sun dipped, I was alone with Belinda: the two of us standing in the garden as if lost, with Groping Head rising up to the sky in the background.

"You're thinking of selling this place, aren't you?" asked Belinda. I reached for her hand.

Later that summer, as a family, we began taking long walks around the headland and eating devon and tomato sauce or ham and mustard sandwiches for dinner on the yellow sand at Little Wobbygong Beach. One evening I arrived home late to find a note from Belinda telling me they'd already left and to meet them at the beach.

By the time I arrived, my family had eaten dinner. Belinda said she'd take the boys along the old path that they loved so much. My daughter waited with me while I ate. Together we looked out to sea, and over towards Groping Head. She talked, I nodded. I put my head back on the blanket and felt the sand give slightly under the weight.

"I'm going to put my feet in, Dad."

"Okay. Just your feet," I said, not opening my eyes, drifting off, almost to sleep.

When I glanced up moments later to check on her, my eyes opened to look right into the setting sun. I turned abruptly away at the sting of it. It was then I saw Aunt Mavis. She moved between the water and me. Younger than I ever knew her, her light brown hair blew in the southeasterly wind, and her figure was full under a long summer dress. Seeing me, she gathered her dress in her hands and lifted it up over her head, letting it drop in the sand. Now in a blue and white striped neck-to-knee bathing suit, she faced me, laughing: her face tanned, her youth newly found. I held onto gravity, she levity, and we traded a wordless moment that was ripe and unfamiliar before she swept down to the water's edge, joining my daughter.

Behind them the sea was pale blue and the windblown breakers were white. The gold sand stretched itself across the foreground of this picture, and the cliffs of Groping Head reflected the oranges and pinks of the setting sun. This was the scene. It would always be this way. The young woman and little girl holding hands as they leapt about playfully, at the mock terror brought on by the shoreline waves.

LYREBIRD

The once-plentiful lyrebird, with the arrival of settlers became the victim of mass slaughter, both for the fun of the hunt and for the commercialisation of the tail feathers, and possibly came close to extinction.

— *Every Australian Bird, Illustrated*

S TARK WHITE BARK, limbs straight or gnarled, worked into a denseness which, when broken by shafts of sun, cut through this bushland like blades. She would appear in a shadow, then vanish in the light. Then appear once more, farther away, grinning with lit-up teeth and creamy eyeballs. She existed as if the dark were light and the light, dark.

She is a remembrance from the old days. Back when no one knew where me and me brother, Little Johno, went of an afternoon after fence building. And who'd care? Pa and the men would climb on horses and ride the long trail to drink with some other men at a shack along the way to Parramatta. For us, there were half a day left over. What joy! Auntie Sarah and Ma were working at home with our older sis, but us, if we stayed away good, we'd not be missed. "Collectin' firewood!" we'd say with a chortle upon our return, as the sky would fill up with orange and pink before settling on such blackness as is its way out here.

Little Johno was two years younger than was I, but he could ride fair and so we would take "old ma" — that was how we called the old mare — and trot along past the outer fences. We'd pretend the land was our own, for it would be one day, so said Pa. We'd lean against its roughness and test the tension of the wire like Pa and the other men would do as when they were building its very self.

She would appear only if we were quiet. The horse tied to a fencepost, Li'l Johno and me would walk along the creek until we came to the pale green rock. If she were about, it was then she would show herself. She would appear first as a lyrebird, a blur in the bush, half running half flying. And we's would follow.

We knew the blacks came and went. Pa would tell us to be mindful of 'em. Don't get too close. Leave 'em be to their own business, he'd say. And so we knew, like such things are meant to be vagaries that sometimes they would be about, sometimes not.

We'd claimed our land fair. These were Pa's words. He'd been emancipated. Here since the early days. His plot, gotten from the crown. Our people had some well-earned respect about these parts and it was due to Pa's diligent management of the land. Never gone hungry once, had we. Pa would always caution to be minding yer own business. It'd got him far, and they were words to live by, he reckoned.

If we ran, she would disappear altogether, or else she would remain as a lyrebird. Creep then, and we would get after her slow. Creep with rather quick little steps so as not to make her vanish, but also so as not to lose sight of her. It were a game, a child's game, now I am to look back on it. She would lead us about the bush in a wide circle that would leave us about where it was that we began. There was a sense of delight to it. Little Johno loved the game.

He would always want to go and find her. Months would pass where we would check for her, but nothing. Then, on a day exactly like the one before it, she would appear and the creeping would begin. The flash white of her smile. We never saw any other of her people. Just her own self. I know now they must have been about. Watching us playing with her, as we watch a pup, blind with newness as it paws at the air, chasing its own tail or the shadow of its tail.

About the time of my tenth birthday we stopped our game. I have always figured Little Johno may have gone once or twice more to look for her. Maybe he found her on his own, the game continuing on without me. I never spoke of it with Little Johno — for he were shot dead at fifteen. A silence passes between brothers as they move into manhood. Secrets of boyhood are sealed shut. Not referred to, ever. Little Johno and me, that were how it happened to us.

It were very early, cold, a frost sheet had settled on the boards of our verandah. Little Johno, fifteen, and I seventeen stood with Pa as he received the news.

"John, git yer horses. We're ridin' after 'em darkies," said the lieutenant himself, his red coat unbuttoned, his chest bared and slick with sweat and dirt, his ribs heaving as he breathed.

Upriver, cows had been stolen by the blacks. What happened then? Well, it were a day like no other. Ordinary men became swept up with rage. For months there were a drought and blacks had been stealing settlers' food. Some were shot dead as punishment. In retaliation, they attacked farms at night and a settler's boy were killed, speared through the guts, some have said! Now, cow thievery.

"We'd been granted this land fair," I said to Pa as we gathered the horses.

It was then he turned to me, and grabbed me clear by the throat. "You, son, were never in chains. You have been granted nothing." Then, in a whisper, his spittle, hard breath next to my face, "*You* have lost nothing."

Following my Pa, Little Johno and I cantered into the group of farmers; some I recognized, some I'd never seen before. Thirty men I reckoned, the horses toey, biting at each other, the men much the same.

"Out there, hiding in the bush, black fellas are feasting on our cattle this very minute — let's ride now!" cried one man.

"Butchering our future, every last bit of it," cried another.

I were there as they raged, pressed, provoked. I must confess my blood boiled as hot as did theirs.

We rode. Us farmers, the corps, some police, too. We met up with others. Then split up in many different directions. For three days and nights Little Johno and I journeyed into the bush and back. The longer we were out, the more hardened did our speaking become. Just what we would do. Just how they would be shown.

I were in the rear as we approached that dreaded clearing. Two shots rang out. Li'l Johno fell from his horse to the dirt. Then more shots. Then there were a scream, an unearthly scream of terror and impossible pain. It were from the mouth of a black, and sounded so human as to have been screamed in English proper. A soldier had a foot on this fellow's chest, grabbed his hair in his fist. He were hacking off the head at the neck with a short axe — the way we might work on a stump for a fencepost.

Yet, I ran to my own brother's side. He were on a mat of leaves, his horse standing at his side, its head bobbing up and down. Johno's mouth were open, saying words too quiet for me to hear. Then none. No words. As his soul left his earthly body the expression on his face were one of uncertainty. How could a loving God let this be?

"He's dead," a man cried, looking down on Johno's body, me holding the weight of it in my arms, at my own heaving chest. "This lad is dead!"

This call began the battle proper. About me men fired shots, and from behind trees and rocks the blacks came and one after another they fell, shot by shot. Bitter gunsmoke and the sweet smell of blood filled the air. I dragged Johno's body to a tree then climbed back onto my horse. I followed the others around a hill and we narrowed in on a group of their women and babes. Seeing us, they ran. We shot, chased, beat. They too all fell. Did I want revenge? I do not know, even now. I were not myself, and that is all. Not human, as I cut at the air, screaming, laughing. Yes, laughing, this hoarse, gleeful laugh that I have never heard come from myself since.

They were all but dead when I saw a small one run off into the bush. I followed it, where I came upon another group of them who had lain in hiding. I hunted after them, joined by other men now. With some difficulty we rounded them up — their backs at a clifftop with nowhere to flee. Women, and little ones. Fifteen or so, for I counted. Bare, mouths open, dusty, confused. There were four of us. Three militiamen and myself.

The corporal dismounted and approached one woman. There were nothing but silence now — she absent of expression — as he ran her lengthwise with his long knife. It were the most awful sight. Her spilling her insides. His hand and coat bloody; almost immediately, flies descended at the warmth of her.

"See. Our bloody cattle in those gizzards," did the corporal scream. His face alarmed, thrilled, he rushed at the others. He were suffering the madness now, too, the sweet taste of death at his lip.

Stopping before more of them, the corporal was about to swing his knife at a small boy. Then one woman amongst them spoke. Her words seem to ring, lengthening the moment. She did not look at me. Nor, I should expect, remember me. But I knew it were her. Her creamy eyes older now but the same white teeth. And her words, her words, it became known, were instructions. For the small group of them, so as to avoid the same fate as the first, turned to the empty sky, and one by one — some carrying small ones, others singularly — leapt off, escaping as easily as lyrebirds, into the valley below.

INSIDE AN INK
CLOUD

S HANE'S ARM WORKED in hard tight circles, topping up the beads of wax spread across the fibreglass face of his surfboard. The Australian winter chilled the sand and it clung to his feet, slowing the blood, making his legs ache right through the skin and muscle to the bones. Shane glanced at his younger brother, Gavin, standing next to him. As Shane zipped up his red-and-white wetsuit and fastened the Velcro flap tight around his neck, Gavin did the same. His little brother had been copying his ways now for longer than he could remember. It was something he made himself ignore at times, lest it irritate him.

Shane's fingers stretched the wetsuit's rubber collar and followed the neckline along, between rubber and skin. A seagull squawked. He put his head back down and continued working the circles. Barely visible through the layer of wax on his board, an octopus peered up at Shane. In looping bulbous letters shaped and stylized like long-lost free love, its tentacles spelled out —

Ink Cloud Surfboards
custom made
since 1970

Beyond the breaking surf a larger set of humps rolled in off the horizon, a serpent. Out there, "out the back" as the boys referred to it, the first wave of the set broke, crashing with a boom — louder, harder than the even thumping Shane had heard up until then.

It interrupted the rhythmic trance of his waxing circles. The serpent's second hump relaxed into the water unexploded, but the third was full and cocked. Shane stood. As if he were an indolent shadow, Gavin, too, rose to his feet seconds later.

Through the early morning half-light Shane analyzed, dissected, partitioned the wave, the way it stood up, how it pitched, the rushing section, the soundless barrel. *The wind could be more westerly*, he thought. *The serpent, she wants hot wind off the back of the Simpson Desert to coax her out of the sea, Shane, to make her stand tall and roar.* This was his stepfather's voice now in his head, the voice that accompanied him whenever he surfed.

"W-wanna go," said Gavin, his board under his arm, taking the first few steps towards the ocean. "I reckon it's light enough." Shane reached down and picked up his board with one hand, ignoring his younger brother. The board, "the harpoon," was a heavy old gun that had lost its sparkle long ago.

"A great w-winter board," Gavin would often tell Shane, echoing their stepfather. "It used to be S-Simon Anderson's board." Simon Anderson had been Gavin's childhood hero, the world champion in seventy-seven, or was it seventy-eight? Shane sucked at history. What he did know was that the board was a hand-me-down heirloom, his only inheritance from his dead stepfather, not Simon Anderson's at all. He kept the truth to himself.

It's been five years since his stepfather was alive. To Shane it seemed like yesterday, but he was only fourteen back then — Gavin's age now. When the surf picked up, when there were serpents to be hunted, they would unsheathe the harpoon. It was stored for such occasions up in the rafters of Shane's uncle's garage. Shane could still feel his stepfather's hands tight on his hips as he hoisted Shane up into the roof. *Grab hold of that joist. Lower it down slowly, Shane. Careful mate, careful not to ding her.* "Serpents," "harpoons," these words — along with the board itself — were all he had left of his stepfather now. He preferred not to think about it, just to listen to his stepfather's words. And he only talked when Shane surfed. So Shane surfed as often as he could.

When Shane was a few years younger, he had a chance to turn Pro-Am. Some said he was that good. Gavin did. Shane was a left-hander, a goofy-foot, tall with strong legs. He had a re-entry that all but snapped the sound barrier, carved long even lines and always shredded fast sections. He was well known, locally, for surfing The Island one July when it was pumping.

"Pumping, Christ! I was there," Gavin would say. "The Island w-was grinding fifteen-foot left-handers that were s-sucking dry to rock and Shane rode one that peeled for ten whole minutes. Right into the beach. Might'a gone all the w-way to the river mouth if he thought he could have paddled back out to catch another one." Shane knew none of this was true, none of it except the part about Gavin having been there.

"I can s-see the horizon getting lighter," Gavin said now. Shane turned his face to find the wind. On top of the dark headland stood a few weatherboard houses, but mainly flats and units, all with panoramic sea views. They had names like The Nor-easterly, The Captain Cook, and The Seabreeze. Retired widows and war veterans lived there. Their carless garages were full of surfboards, a great convenience for their beach-going grandchildren. For them, the oldies, the boards in their garages were insurance that they'd receive young visitors, tired and hungry after a long morning battling the surf. Their buildings were well-maintained and sported harshly trimmed gardens with hearty plants and healthy grass. It was to these manicured preoccupations that Shane now focused his attention. He began by picking out familiar trees and leaves. He spotted the sparse garden of The Seabreeze. Nothing moved. Then, over to the far right, on the very edge of the cliff, ever so slightly, an oleander swayed.

At this signal, Shane and Gavin jogged into the surf. The August sea was so cold that their feet grew numb. Shane picked a line to paddle out through the surf. The walls of whitewater, the angry, thundering waves approached him, only to be silenced as he sank his board under the water and duck-dived, slipping beneath each of them without losing ground. Between the sets he paddled hard. Gavin, on a light, short board, could not keep pace and the swell and rip tossed him back to shore.

Once out the back, Shane sat straddling the board, floating, waiting. He forced circles in the water with his arms, turning. He saw Gavin standing on the beach. Shane glanced over to his left. Now the oleanders danced and swooned in the warm westerly wind, luring, charming the serpent out of her sea. He drew more circles in the water and faced the horizon.

Shane saw clouds at such a distance they may as well have been hanging over New Zealand, or Chile. These clouds, in a sky the consistency of black ink, became holes, or watermarks; the more Shane stared, the more they looked like negatives of themselves. And the orange light that sprang from far below the horizon in thin threads disappeared behind these holes.

Shane sensed a set rolling in. He put his head down and paddled out, pushing water behind him, his arms pistons. The third wave along the serpent's back was the one he hunted, the one with the fullest shape and the greatest bounty. Paddling, Shane wanted to get so close to her power he could stare her in the face, ride so far back in the tube, be so covered by her, that he could forget himself.

As the first wave passed under him and the second wave stood before him, Shane sank into the trough, a heart-quickening space where he was unable to see the beach or the horizon. A private place, between walls of water, windless, hidden from as far as the eye can see. Then, like a fleeting smile, through the curling face of the approaching wave shot a dark shape — a porpoise or shark, an inky shadow on a cave wall made of water.

Shane turned and paddled, panicking, forcing his arms to enter the water. The second wave sank and disappeared almost underneath him. The third wave was now in view; he was out of place. Stranded too close to shore, he paddled hard, back out, towards the oncoming wave. The sky lightened to deep blue. *So what*, he told himself, *if it is a shark it's probably all gums. A toothless wonder.* That's what his stepfather would have said.

Shane's stepfather had been bitten by a shark. Had 250 stitches from his knee to his back. *It was all gums*, he would say, during the next three months in the hospital. *The shark took three goes at getting a good hold and gave up. Seems I wasn't tasty enough for him.* His stepfather had fallen off a wave; the shark took him in knee-high surf. He died finally of "complications." The thing was, no one had expected him to hang on, to fight a losing battle for his life for anywhere near three months; only recently did Shane discover this. At the time, his stepfather's death had come as a complete shock to Shane.

He had thought hospitals were places where people got better.

Now, the third wave towered over Shane and in the poor light he couldn't grasp her reach. Late takeoff. The nose of Shane's board pointed straight down at the sandbar fourteen feet below. His arms were above his head, his feet not sticking to the board. He tried to bottom turn, but fell, into the rising wave that then sucked him up through the face, and tossed him over the falls. *Rushed wax job*, thought Shane, tumbling in the white water, his board flinging about him, attached to his ankle by a neon-orange leg rope. *When you have no control in the surf, when you can't take a breath, mate, don't fight it. Just go limp, enjoy it.* His stepfather's voice, clear and firm.

The board's tail momentarily dug into the sand and the sharp nose stabbed a twirling Shane in the upper thigh, ripping right through wetsuit and skin and muscle. The impact snapped the leg rope and broke the board in half. To Shane it felt like a dull thump, not like a shark bite at all.

From the beach, Gavin didn't see the fall. The darkness, the pitching wave, the foreground foam all helped to obstruct his view. He waited, and waited. Then he spotted half of Shane's board.

When Shane finally appeared, lurching about in knee-high water, Gavin ran to drag his brother out.

"My bum is killing me," said Shane. On the shore, Gavin saw the rip in the wetsuit, but no blood.

"Oh, Shane, you're going to be pissed off." Shane's wetsuit was new. It had taken him two months to save up for it on his apprentice's wages. Gavin parted the rubber flaps and looked inside at Shane's leg. "Sh-shit, you're cut, mate," said Gavin, and to protect Shane from his own shock, Gavin turned his head away. "But don't worry, the salt water is good for cuts." Gavin drew in several deep breaths.

Shane's fingers probed down into the tear in his wetsuit. His index finger felt numb meat. He remembered the smile across the wave's face. He'd seen his stepfather's body just days after the shark attack. The threads of stitched skin and tissue, orange disinfectant, black bruises had never faded in his mind. A seagull squawked. Shane collapsed, face first, in the sand.

Gavin forced all his fingers through the gash in the wetsuit to clamp the two loose halves of Shane's upper leg together, wanting to hide the white bone he could see. Although Shane remained alert, his leg was deadened, and he was ignorant of Gavin's supporting clutch. Shane kept his eyes closed. The cool sand cradled and soothed his head. For a while, he imagined eating breakfast with his uncle at The Seabreeze, looking out over the sea. And, although Gavin was not present in his daydream, he could hear Gavin narrating the scene in his customary fits and starts, telling a long story about a wave they once rode together, side by side.

Down the beach, the top half of Shane's board washed up onto the sand. The foam core lay exposed, white in contrast to the board's sun-dulled fibreglass skin. On the surface, under the layer of wax, the octopus stared up at the sky. Its tentacles wound out the words:

Ink Cloud Surfboards
custom made

in looping bulbous letters shaped and stylized like long-lost free love.

DESPITE   ·
LAST NIGHT'S
RAIN

·

January 26th, 1988 (Australia Day)

AS GEORGE AND JANE ENTERED The Seabreeze, George inspected the fountain gurgling away to itself in the foyer. Someone's kids had cleaned out the silver coins — leaving only a few greening coppers. George disliked the foyer for its humidity and décor. He'd always felt passing through it was rather like floating in an outmoded public aquarium. It had fish motifs etched into every other tile, themselves coloured in various shades of swimming-pool blue. It inevitably reminded George of that cheap holiday in Blackpool years ago. Nothing more than a two-day respite from relatives during their one and only trip back home, to England. He tossed a copper wish in the fountain and cursed the day they had moved to this block of flats, leaving their house on the clifftop farther down the esplanade.

Jane stepped into the elevator, but George climbed the stairs. He didn't like little rooms, and who could trust an old elevator's cables? On the stairs George reflected briefly on the afternoon's events. They'd been watching the Australian bicentennial celebrations on the television at Jane's sister Emma's place. Emma's two boys had not been home. Off surfing, Emma had mentioned when they'd arrived.

Once inside their flat, Jane began the preparations for dinner by getting four sausages out of the freezer. George sat on the balcony and watched the last few surfboard riders catching waves out off the semi-submerged reef.

"Is it too dark?" Jane asked through the screen door.

"I'm looking for them. I think I might see one of the boys. Isn't one of their wetsuits blue and red?"

"Why don't I call Emma and see if either of the boys would come round tomorrow for breakfast? Would you like that?"

At dusk from his old house George had often stared over at the national park. From his old garden he used to watch the eroding pink and orange sandstone cliffs across the mouth of the river, crowned with blazing wildflowers, gold and crimson bottlebrushes, blue gums and hardy scrub. Sometimes at dusk when the light danced off the water into the silvery leaves, George had half expected to see a black man emerge from the bush, hunting, holding a spear, boomerang, and woomera — an ancient aboriginal man, a fugitive, who had somehow managed to stay hidden and preserved for these two hundred years. George had considered his old view to be that authentic, that Australian. But all that was visible from his balcony here at The Seabreeze were the stacks from the oil refinery smoking behind a distant beach.

George could hear Jane talking on the phone to Emma. None of the surfers out this late appeared to be the boys. There was a time, he thought, he might have wanted sons. But thirty years ago Dr. Northcliffe had said plain and simple: *George, mate, I reckon your wife's barren.*

So that had always been that.

George unlaced his brogues, took off his socks and rubbed his old feet. Boys of his own, he thought. And although he couldn't quite place it, what he sensed in the night air was the beginning of rain. As he dozed off to sleep, the last surfboard rider paddled into shore and clouds gathered along the horizon. George dreamed himself holding Emma, at his old house with his view, and her two sons by their side. They all stood in the garden, bare toes in the dry soil, holding onto the wire fence. Like a family, they looked over the cliff's edge to the rock shelf below, down to where Jane lay.

December 19th, 1977. Christmas shopping, Sydney

IN MYERS DEPARTMENT STORE, the virile young mannequins — with their cocked heads and self-righteous grins — looked down on middle-aged George like he was half the man they were. On the escalator, walls of mirrors fenced him in for his entire ascension: one thousand peripheral versions of himself, in profile, each trying to ignore the existence of the next. He felt his private world being exposed — like a felt hat punched inside out — for all the other shoppers to see.

It was a mannequin in men's wear who began the chiding. A youth, frozen in mid-athletic-stride, said: *George, this is your life, there's no way out, mate.*

George began to perspire. And then another started, a petrified face, barely old enough to vote: *Pay no attention to him George, but believe me! You will be the last man in your family's line. Why, this is the fall of the house of George,* he laughed.

Then, in chorus, the whole room full of mannequins chanted:

The fall of the house of George,
by George,
the fall of the house of George!

"Stop it." George said this aloud without meaning to.

"Stop what?" Jane groped for his hand without taking her eyes off a fresh pile of corduroy slacks. She continued: "George, dear, are you hungry?" He took her hand.

George looked to his feet for stability. His Sunday shoes. Solid black brogues. In order to escape, he tried to think of something real, his house, his view, the half-finished Jane Austen novel beside his bed. But what of his ride on top of the toothy, free-spirited, wooden stair? The mannequins, the mirrors, the escalators? He could trust nothing in this world, not his own sanity, not gravity, not English novels, not even his Sunday shoes — as it was, after all, only Saturday.

Since Emma and her sons immigrated to Australia two years ago, George had felt Jane's spirits rise. He welcomed this. He did. But, shopping for children, here in the city? Especially now, after that new surfer-husband of Emma's had gone and got himself attacked by a shark. They said he might not make it.

George, who was now outside walking down Martin Place, felt the buildings teetering around him, the clouds moving because the skyscrapers were falling. With every step he confronted a precipice. He looked down, and letting his mind wander, George jettisoned himself from his body, his clothes and brogues, and imagined himself in his garden, cooking fish over coals. He regarded Jane at her garden looking over the wire fence, to the rocks and sea below. The smell of bream cooking, sea salt and gum trees all bled together and soothed his mind and mood. The two boys played cricket and Emma stood by his side, her hand inside his. Together they watched the horizon. George's gait widened, his speed increased down Martin Place. He licked his lips.

"Oh, honey look, lamingtons." Jane released George's hand and ducked into a pastry shop. A little brass bell rang overhead. She approached the glass counter and bowed, studying the cakes, pastries, pies, slices, biscuits, tarts.

"What do you think of those lamingtons there, George?" She placed her index finger on the glass, showing him.

"Excuse me, Lovey?" The woman behind the counter asked.

Jane looked up. The elderly woman's accent was English, from the North like her own. Jane took in her questioning face for a second, then followed the woman's gaze back over her own shoulder. Jane had been talking to herself. There was no one else in the shop. No George.

George had released his wife's hand without a thought. The fish on the barbecue seared away, the ocean wind swept through his hair, and over the mirrored seascape the sun danced off the tiny wispy brush strokes, the wave crests, the dabs of white paint only characterizing foam, only implying the true nature of things.

It was not until George reached Pitt Street that he returned to the city, his clothes, brogues, and situation. It was a car horn that snapped him out of it. Like a bridge of sound, the horn carried him the sixty kilometres back to himself in an instant, and with a thud.

"Watch it, mate. Bit early for the drink, don't you reckon?" asked a voice. George turned, staggering and falling, but the bloke who said this could have been any one of the grey suits that were now stepping around him.

With his freshly shaven face against the smooth, hot cement, George forgot himself, lost Emma's touch, misplaced his view of the sea. He was alive, yes, he was sure of it. But whose life was he inside of? What if he'd become a local: a man who could not live without overlooking the sea, a Sydneysider who needed the flat horizon, the distant bush, and the wind-battered cliffs simply to feel whole? Was he no longer British; was he now, an Australian?

George considered this new unfortunate life sentence by punishing sentence.

Cheek. Hot.

Then, slowly, awkward clothes arrived, a pair of stiff shoes, some noise. He was becoming himself. He felt foreign again. He felt English.

"George, dear, you've collapsed in the middle of the side-walk." It was Jane's voice, urgent but reassuring nonetheless.

Back in the pastry shop, they ate curried egg sandwiches in a small booth. George drank a vanilla milkshake. Jane sipped tea. They shared a lamington. It was all the walking. It was the heat. On an empty stomach, indeed. And it was Christmas. Goodness, so much shopping to do. Well, they wouldn't come into Sydney next year. The train fare was too dear, and really they could get the boys' gifts at the Walton's nearby. It was a good store. They have everything you'd want to give and get for Christmas — much of it on sale, too.

Jane held George's hand. She was doing all the talking. He liked it when she talked. Her voice ran through him and soothed his mind like a scotch and water. Jane had been a nurse when they'd met. She still knew how to diagnose and disinfect.

On the train home, George began to relay his day to Jane. What had happened to him, the mannequins' voices in Myers, the flight home to the sea. But the sight of the river running underneath an oncoming bridge reassured him that he would soon be at home; so he stopped shy of telling her it all. During this silence George regained some strength, found some sense, and made the towering heights of Pitt Street, the loathsome temperature of the day, and the indefatigable noise of the city drop away from his mind.

A week after the incident, his recollection of his fall was only partial. Two years later it was unsalvageable.

Summer's end, 1975. Beefeater Gin, Indian tonic water, two sisters.

"THE SEA HAS NO PASSION." Jane hunched over and lit a cigarette. There was wind. "It's barren and that is why, millions of years ago, we all slithered out."

"Then why live so near to it, on a clifftop?" Emma asked.

"Struth, as they say here. It's an island. Water, water everywhere. Why live anywhere in Australia?"

"Because you must have wanted to, at least at first. But why live on a clifftop?"

"Oh, because *he* wanted to." Jane looked out at the bleeding dusk. She smoked. "It's because George is impossibly dramatic." She paused. "And a verandah on a clifftop could be rather like a stage, I suppose. The whole bloody country — full of actors and actresses performing before the sea as if it's some kind of great audience." She drew on her cigarette, smiling at the sound of her own cleverness there. She'd been aching, she now realized, for her sister, for this familiar sort of conversation.

"But Jane. You've got to be dotty to stay here."

"What? Leave? And let the sea be his only audience, let him become an Australian? I shouldn't think so. We moved here because we wanted a place untouched by war, somewhere with a fresh start for the ripping great life we'd be leading together."

George and Jane had met in London. He was the young schoolmaster on summer holiday. She, the nurse in training on leave from Lancashire. He taught Latin, geography, and cricket. She dressed wounds and liked to garden. He had a moustache and a sunburned nose. She had a long birthmark on her stomach, which — if he looked at it upside down — was the shape of Italy, with the toe of its boot disappearing up under her breast. (An attribute that could only be fully appreciated by a Latin and geography teacher, he'd assured her.)

After a courtship that lasted long enough to sample, but not overindulge in, selected parts of Europe, they motored to Lancashire and were married in a church that was two hundred years older than Australia. That was 1948. April third. Not long after, they purchased a berth on the P&O sailing for Sydney.

"Another?" said Emma reaching for Jane's glass.

"Yes." They met one another's gaze. Four smacking blue eyes with interlocking flecks of British racing green. The Firth sisters from Colne were together again. "George loves your boys, Emma. He treats them like his own. Thank you for coming." Emma, mother of two, recent widower, was the younger sister by almost ten years.

"I knew you would never leave him here. I thought I had to come."

"Cheers, then." They charged their glasses. Jane saw Emma as she had seen herself a decade ago, fresher faced, more able-bodied.

November, 1954. Gardening.

JANE STEPPED OFF THE VERANDAH and crossed their back lawn to her row of vegetables planted along the wire fence at the cliff's edge. Despite last night's rain, the coarse grass, infested with patches of burrs and bindi-eyes, crunched under her sandalled feet, the wetness flicking up on her legs, itching her skin. There lay her "hopefuls": a few sad carrots, a tired pumpkin, an unlikely union of herbs huddling together for mutual protection. It's death row, she thought. They'd surely jump if they had any courage.

Jane squatted and poked her index finger into the earth at the foot of a tomato plant. Dry. There had been good rain last night; but she knew the sandy soil lacked depth. Besides, she thought, to plants this exposed, the southerly busters are merciless on anything shorter than a small boy. And the sun and salt contribute to — well, they just contribute. She rubbed the waxy skin of a green tomato on its vine, and it snapped off.

The door banged behind George as he considered stepping out across the lawn.

"That tomato ripe already?" he called from the verandah. She watched the wet, uncut grass seducing his bare feet. A vacant moment passed before he found what she called his "take-charge face." He marched over to her, his strides measured and sure, the grass licking at his ankles.

"I picked it, accidentally," she said as he drew near.

"If you pop it on the windowsill, it'll ripen in the sun." George looped his arm inside Jane's and held her hand, adding, "Won't it." George looked out at the morning sun. "It's going to be a humid one today, yeah?" She didn't answer. He turned and looked over at the national park, his eyes combing the bush for movement of any kind.

"Nothing grows here," said Jane as she handed the green tomato to George.

"My carrots were good last year."

"George, please. You've still not told me what Dr. Northcliffe said yesterday when he rang back?"

"Oh, just to keep at it." George gave his wife a reassuring squeeze. He handed her back the green tomato.

"Put that on the kitchen windowsill." Then he turned and retraced his steps back across the grass that was already beginning to dry.

She did not move. From where she stood, the top strand of the thin wire fence clumsily followed the horizon's line. She remained fixed there, before her garden, on the clifftop alongside her hopefuls, waiting for better rain that was sure to come.

GLASS PAPER

SOMETHING WAS MISSING. Keith hesitated in the doorway of their bedroom. He carried a wicker breakfast tray. On it lay a peeled orange, a cup of well-steeped raspberry tea with lots of sugar, and two slices of very toasted toast with just a skerrick of real butter and honey. He retraced his steps to the kitchen, put down the tray, thought for a moment, then he popped out to a neighbour's garden to snip a flower. He plopped a hibiscus into a half-glass of water and placed it on the tray. And from the fridge — as a green afterthought — he added some spearmint leaves. Keith returned to the bedroom, and gently spoke:

"Edwina, would you like some tea?"

Through the window slats a rainbow broke into the bedroom in crisp lines. Keith watched the dust dance and whirl in the light shafts, glistening like stars and comets spiralling out of their orbits. Edwina lay on her side on the bed — pregnant, naked — with tiny chaotic specks raining down on her stomach. It looked to Keith as if her stomach were as big as the entire world. For a brief moment, Keith began to think about someone else. He stopped himself.

He placed the breakfast tray beside Edwina on the bed and sat, focusing on his sleeping wife.

"I'll be at the store all morning. Inventory. Might go to an auction, after lunch." Keith's eyes fell over her glowing skin: my china with gold guilt. "But I'll have my phone with me. This afternoon." Then he added, "I'll call you." Keith waited for

Edwina's eyes to open. "So the tray. Honey. It's tea and toast. With honey, Honey. Like you like it." Now she nodded, slightly.

He reached into his pocket to check for reminder notes. He found one. "Oh, I almost forgot. Remember your idea for the self-portrait...well, yesterday at the store I found something for you to use. Only if you like it. I left it in your studio."

Yesterday, in an attempt at cleaning up the shop before he left for the day, Keith had loaded the van with odds and ends: a 1940s globe, a rotted horse bridle, vols. C, L, and T of an early leather-bound Encyclopaedia set, an old cricket bat autographed by many of the English players from the bodyline series, and an interesting pine window frame. He had thought that Edwina might like the frame. She could paint something in four parts, replacing the glass panes. It could be for the self-portrait she's been talking about. Maybe four scenes from her life, or something. So as not to forget, Keith had jotted down on a slip of paper: *window — self-portrait — four parts*, and popped it into his jacket pocket.

"I love you, Keith," Edwina said, her lips parting to a slit, her eyes still closed. Her breath sent the dust scattering, cleaning out the light shafts. Keith regarded her round belly for a moment, a porcelain pattern, thin blue flowers trickling down ribbed bone china. Under direct sunlight, upside-down, the flower chains looked like veins. Then a cloud blocked the sun and the light in the bedroom turned grey. Keith stood and moved the breakfast tray to the bedside table. He left for work, locking the door behind him.

THE SMELL OF THE RASPBERRY TEA enticed Edwina out of sleep. She opened one eye at a time, then scratched her stomach in firm, even, longitudinal lines. It's so bright in here, she thought. Gradually she made her way to the edge of the bed. She rose to a sit, propping herself up on her arms and lowering her feet to the floor — puffy elephant-pad feet. Edwina lifted the cup of tea to her lips and took a sip. As the warm liquid slid down, she saw the green leaves tossed on the side of the plate. Why is he feeding me coriander for breakfast? Then she noticed the hibiscus stem dangling in the water. She laughed, and a salty tear rolled down, over her lips, onto her breast.

"You are so common," she said to Keith, even though he'd left the house ten minutes ago. Common. Her thoughts fluctuated from the word common — a snobbish term her mother used, one she had never used before now — to Keith, in the kitchen, trying so hard to give her simple breakfast a special touch. The funny part was, if he'd found a parsley sprig or even mint leaves, his heartfelt intentions might have remained as unappreciated as a garnish. Here, though, was a tired piece of coriander, and to Edwina this attempt was the fuel of their slow-burning passion. Keith often made forgivable mistakes, like his confusing greens, and these errors had become compacted in her memory — ancient forests turned into seams of coal. She thought of her love like this. The very stuff of life: as elemental as carbon. But compounded somehow, and coveted by others. Lucrative, rich and dense.

KEITH SPENT THE BETTER PART of his morning reading up on the history of silver inkstands because a young woman telephoned Clayton & Son Antiques wanting to sell her grandmother's collection. Keith felt he was a little weak in the area

of inkstands, indeed in silverware in general. He had a good eye
for furniture, and was trustworthy counsel on porcelain. For
years he had had a personal interest in antiquarian books, but
he was weak in silverware. *Know thy maker's marks* — old words
of his father's he'd failed to live by. He knew there was no choice
but to ring.

"Dad, inkstands. What do you know?" Old Gerry Clayton
loved two things in life: his collection of Irish silver (mainly
dishrings and butter dishes) and gambling.

"What do I know about, what, inkstands? They used to be
called standishes."

"Really, Dad."

"Only a little. Who wants to know?"

"A woman's coming over with her whole inkstand collection today. Can you come round?"

"I'm playing cards today. Tonight?"

"I'll meet you at the store at six."

The shop was messy and understocked. Since the pregnancy
began, Keith had been less than diligent with his work. Arriving
late, leaving early, missing auctions, accepting junk on con-
signment. He looked around the room. Dad's going to croak,
thought Keith, if he sees the shop like this.

Keith closed the books on silverware and inkstands and
began dusting, moving furniture, collecting up the worthless
stuff and moving it into a pile by the back door. He felt this
pregnancy was using up all his time. His father had bet him as
much would happen.

ON THE EDGE OF HER BED Edwina ate her toast and finished her tea. In the bathroom she soaked a facecloth in warm water and sponged herself down. Back in the bedroom she slipped on a summer dress that looked more like a parachute than clothing. She wandered downstairs into her studio.

A large mural done in watercolours hung across the far wall. It was a present, a collaboration done for Edwina by her Year One class. The picture was filled with suspended figures of primary-coloured babies, done at all angles; intentional umbilical cords were entangled with accidental drips and dribbles. Along the bottom in perfect substitute-teacher cursive was, *Good luck, Ms. Underwood, we miss you teaching us how to paint — class 1C.* At this, she laughed and cried. For God's sake, she thought, when will I stop crying at everything? She grabbed a handful of parachute and dabbed her eyes, still laughing at one of her kids whose baby had only three fingers on one hand, and an umbilical cord that ran out of its mouth. Then she stopped laughing altogether. She must get going today. Do something. Keep her mind working.

When Edwina saw Keith's pile of junk in the middle of the studio floor she remembered her husband's words: "Your self-portrait idea... yesterday at the store I found something." She hadn't believed him. How apt, how insightful, how unlike Keith.

"Well, we'll have fun with you, won't we," said Edwina as she picked up the globe and rested it on her stomach, spinning it between her fingers. Then she placed it on her worktable and pulled the other junk — the books, the bat, the harness, and the old, broken, pine windowframe — right out of the room.

For the last month or so, when Edwina worked she sat on a fat cushion on the ground, with her back against a wall, her paints and other supplies spread out around her. Had she been off teaching for a month? She'd named this position her "working picnic" and this is how, after some manoeuvring, she ended up today. Edwina gathered a bag of cloth end-pieces, a box of scrap paper, and a set of watercolours and inks. She regarded the old globe, spinning it slowly with her fingers: Abyssinia, French West Africa, Sargasso Sea, Melanesia, Sumatra, Ceylon.

In a chipped bone china teacup, Edwina poured a little starch, some corn flour and, with a spoon, she trickled in water and began to work and fold together the ingredients, making paste. At the bottom of the bag of cloth scraps she found a triangle of lime-green cotton. It was from the bolt of fabric her mother had bought to use at their wedding as a backdrop for the band. Great band. She remembered Keith in his tuxedo, his father's watch fob and cufflinks. She smoothed on the paste with her index finger, covering the green triangle evenly, and then she turned it over and hung one tip on Iceland, running her thumb down the edge to Bulgaria, then over to Gibraltar, and back up to Iceland. It covered Europe.

In the box, Edwina found a piece of glass paper she'd used at art school to complete a project. A group of them had carved a modernist totem pole — a wooden tower of TVs, cars, alarm clocks, advertising icons — out of a dead Norfolk pine in a park near the school. It took them months of hard work, and once she'd stayed up all night on the scaffolding, sanding. Mike Furey stayed with her, sometimes sanding, mostly playing harmonica and making her laugh. This piece of glass paper she fixed over British Columbia, Canada, because they'd read so many books, looked at so many totem poles of the coastal peoples who lived there, she and Mike. Last she'd heard, Mike Furey was married and he'd moved to Western Australia, to Broome of all places.

Edwina pasted bits of rice paper, red velvet, hemp, felt, and denim wherever they fit. By lunch she held a quilted sphere, a patchwork world, and she stood up and went to the kitchen to make a raspberry tea and wait for the paste to dry.

She spent the afternoon with her globe, painting tiny water-colour scenes overlapping looping spirals, joining pieces of cloth to paper, to words that seeped through in thin oceanic names, and bled into endless maternal motifs. With reed dipped in ink, she made sketches of a body, its latitudes showing a divisive, jagged, international dateline that remained partially erased by her reconstruction, but nonetheless there, like the idea of a caesarean scar, and how even it would heal, should things come to that.

The finished globe sat proudly before her by dusk. *My Equations of Time,* she called it. Edwina carried her self-portrait out to the verandah and placed it on the table, to show Keith the minute he came home.

THE YOUNG WOMAN ARRIVED at the shop at closing time: five-thirty. Keith let her in and locked the door behind her. She lifted a heavy box onto the desk. Keith opened the lid and lifted out the first inkstand.

"Why is your grandmother selling her collection?" The woman was perhaps eighteen, maybe twenty. Keith felt uneasy buying articles from people other than their owners.

"She's moved into a nursing home. She doesn't have enough room now." He unpacked most of the box's contents onto the table. Keith regarded the young woman's hands. She was fidgeting, twisting her thumb ring over and over. Her arms were brown. She had grease embedded in the fine folds of her knuckles. Around her neck hung a silver chain. Her T-shirt was pulled tight across her breasts and stopped right above her navel, leaving a hand's width of brown flesh exposed. Keith leaned in, reaching into the box, his head down, but his eyes gazing up at her sunken navel, at her taut flat stomach.

"Can you excuse me for a moment?" Keith walked into the back room and called his father.

"Oh, Dad, you're still there."

"I'm coming, I'm coming."

"No, don't come. That's why I'm calling. She's here. It's all junk."

"Okay, then, Son."

"Thanks anyway, Dad."

Keith returned to the front of the store to find the young woman right where he'd left her, up against the counter, lost in her own thoughts.

"Hi," said Keith as he approached. "I'm afraid there's not much here. This one is sellable." He picked up an inkstand made of glass and metal; it had a crest on the front and an engraving that read *President 1940*. "This crest is from one of the big private clubs in Sydney. Some old bloke might like it."

"How much?" She looked at him hard in the eyes, her hands restless.

"I could give you thirty dollars for it. But the rest really are just souvenirs ..."

"Shit, shit, shit." She began to swear under her breath, then, she said: "Oh, I'm dead." Keith came out from behind his desk. "I need five hundred dollars by tomorrow." Keith just stood still. He couldn't help her; her inkstands were worthless. She'd probably stolen them, and he really didn't want to get involved in her affairs.

"I sold my boyfriend's motorbike. I got ripped off. This little prick ripped me off." She sat down on the Victorian day bed behind her and buried her head in her hands. "This time he's going to drop me for good." Her breathing was shallow and rapid, her fingers pulled at her blonde hair. For Keith, just standing there, this continued for a rather long half-minute. Then she said:

"If they *were* worth five hundred, could you pay me it, *now*?" Keith saw a red-faced young woman. He heard the stony seed of desperation caught in her throat.

"Yes." Of course, if they were worth five hundred he'd pay five hundred. Mind you, he'd sell them for three thousand, were that the case. But then the shop fell quiet for a moment, because the many antiques in the narrow room had been around for a good many years, and they could sense the beginnings of a steamy scene.

Keith said nothing more. He just stood with his hands by his sides. But he realised he must have *done* something — a facial muscle must have betrayed him, one of the little ones by the eye, or mouth — because the young woman crossed her arms over her heart and pulled her T-shirt up over her head.

A Victorian daybed is not as bad a place to be seduced for money as one might think, and Keith retained several clear memories from the occasion: he performed like he was being filmed or at least as if someone were watching, but mostly what he remembered was loving every dirty minute of it. He couldn't imagine sharing anything in common with this young woman, but now they had four and a half inerasable minutes. He made a not-negotiable cheque out for five hundred and thirty dollars (she agreed to throw in the crested inkstand.)

As she left, Keith locked the front door behind her. He looked over at the empty Victorian daybed. Late afternoon sunlight flooded in through the window and the heavy dust they'd kicked up danced and whirled about in a cloud of garish spirals. Keith stood for a moment, negotiating, analyzing. He grabbed the crested inkstand, and his keys, and went out back to the van. He drove it straight to his father's. He would call his wife from there.

EDWINA UNDERSTOOD KEITH having to work late, showing stock to his father, discussing the antiques trade. She knew what those two got up to: they'd drink beer like men, then talk about china like women. She'd have a tea and go up to bed; he'd climb in much later.

Her patchwork globe sat in front of her. And once more Edwina thought of Mike Furey. In her mind, the smell of Norfolk pine filled the air and her senses, and she climbed the totem pole for one final time that day. *What is this feeling, a kind of desire, longing?* She wanted, abruptly, to talk. But not to Keith: to someone else. To Mike Furey.

On their small verandah, she waited for the feeling to pass — the glass paper scattering the bright moonlight. As the world spun she watched the light sparkle and then, as it crossed over a border into a neighbouring country, fade. She'd left spaces and gaps, she saw now. But, before long, the light would flicker again on the next piece of glass paper, and begin anew.

LANDMARKS

I CAN TELL YOU THE STORY, but it is more like one of those dreams that recur, coming back from far away when you find yourself asleep in a strange bedroom. At breakfast you are polite, say you slept well as you butter your toast and accept tea as a matter of course when you'd much rather have coffee. The visions linger a little for the morning as you are carted around and shown a good time by your hosts. But they are not visions; they are memories. At least, they are versions of memories. They are like the last hours of a sickness after a fever has broken but the threat of it is fresh, or perhaps they are more like the first hours of it, before you even recognize there is something wrong. Do you know these dreams, then?

Start with two pool lights, one red, one blue. From them, send thin veins of slanted light toward each other from opposite sides of the pool. They cloud the water a dark and unnatural blue — the colour of cold lips. Hear your heart beating. It should be louder than the noise of frantic childhood friends who seem thousands of feet above you. Make the night water thick, heavy, on your chest.

"Marco?" You hear a girl call from the shallow end. It is her, Cassy. Her arms are outstretched, eyes shut tight. She is groping, lurching for a body. What do you do then? This is still a game. You submerge, soundlessly.

Run your fingers over the filter to your left. This is the very deepest point of the pool. Have it suck your hand firmly over the grate. Look at the grid marks left imprinted there; slide it, to get it off. Turn yourself over, look up, see legs and arms kicking and waving above you in a mad summer of youth.

Tease your lungs. Let air trickle out your nose. Have panic set in but control it. Hear a voice: *Come on, you're a world champion.* Work along the bottom like a marine creature. Use your fingers and toes only, a crab. Here's the side, scuttle up the gentle curve. Roll yourself over onto your stomach again, coil, release. Extend your legs and feel yourself blast through the water, straight body, dragless, diagonal to the surface, *three ... two ... one ... touch. World champion underwater swimmer, the man's a legend.* Feel cool night air as it hits your face and the sting of the chlorine as your eyes are opened to the world.

"Polo!" is cried out about you. Say it for me, too, and pencil your body, pull up your arms, and shoot yourself down deep, feet first. Lie flat against the pool's bottom with your cheek against the cement. Listen to the underwater night.

This is the way the story always begins when I dream it.

"IS EVERYONE STILL PLAYING? Somebody?" said Cassy, who'd swum over you, and is now in the deep end where you had begun, only minutes beforehand.

"Yeah?" you answer because you are so far away. Rodney is a metre to her right and is trying not to laugh and be discovered.

"How come I can't catch anyone? Marco?" she says with the beginning of anguish in her voice. You like her in this gentle pain.

"Polo," you cry along with the others.

Most of the gang sits around the edge of the pool with a

finger dangling in. This to escape a well-placed, "Fish out of water!" call. They move only when Cassy comes too close.

"This sucks," says Cassy, opening her eyes. "I'm getting out."

And so the game ends. Everyone walks or rides their bikes home. "Marco Polo" has lost its tactical sting. When you were all younger, you'd have stayed in the water for hours, playing, hugging the bottom in silence. Now it is sometimes hard to even get the girls into the water. You and Rodney used to just throw them in if they said it was too cold. But then your mother yelled to you from the upstairs verandah: "Listen! You too, Rodney Singh. Don't throw any of the girls in the pool. Do you hear me? You're older now and they can't always get wet." We snigger.

That next Saturday afternoon all the girls get in. But you bore quickly and get out.

"Hey, you blokes. Let's play 'catch and kiss,' " says Rodney. You just look at him.

"God, you're immature, Rodney," says Cassy. She has recently discovered that this is a particularly hurtful insult. But Rodney's idea is considered anyway. The next thing you know you are in the garage looking for something so you can play "spin the bottle." This is a close, but in Cassy's estimation, a more mature cousin of catch and kiss.

Minutes later, an empty bottle is spinning and bouncing over the bricks beside the pool. Two by two you march off behind the pool shed and rub noses, bump heads, shake hands, stick fingers in navels and even, on one or two occasions, kiss.

Cassy has long earth-red hair that she can sit on if she throws her head back. You are shorter than she is, so you just stand there petrified, behind the shed, with its filter humming and hot, looking up at a girl who's lived down the road from you for twelve years. She has a new mouthful of braces.

"We don't have to. If you don't wanna," she says. Her wet hair clings to her shoulders like sheets of bark. You notice the shape of her beneath her swimsuit. How all-of-a-sudden she looks.

"All right," you say. Are you relieved? But then she leans forward and does it anyway. Tongue-tips, hair in mouth, steel and lips, held breaths. This feels … these feelings are beyond you. You are in the movies. You are your cool older cousin who does this *all the time*. You have a secret, you have big knowledge, you are entrusted, blessed, anointed. You are also erect. You have to get it down. Nonchalantly.

"Does this mean we're going around with each other?" she asks. Her voice is clear. This is an important question. You are helplessly distracted. You glance down inadvertently. She sees where you look.

The next day, Rodney, you, and the girls get back from the beach after Junior Surf Life Saving lessons. Your Mum makes you go. It's good for you, she says. The sun glares off the bricks around the pool. The whole gang will come over later on for an afternoon swim. Rodney and you play cricket for ages and the girls suntan. Rodney just keeps staring at them.

"Ah, mate, Cassy's tops," says Rodney finally, to see your reaction.

"She's all right," you say. You are cool.

"Tell us what happened yesterday. Did ya crack on to her?"

"Shut up. Bowl, you wanker."

"You're a Cassy-lover."

"Bugger off, Rodney."

"Let it go, you blokes," says Cassy, looking up from her tanning position.

Rodney and you cricket for a while longer. He tries to bowl faster and faster. You try to hit them farther and farther away, to an imaginary deep extra cover, or long off, or deep third man.

"Howzat?" Rodney asks the question. You are gone. The fence on the full is out. House rules. Caught at silly point. You throw down the bat.

Just then, the rest of the gang comes in through the side gate. You walk over to get a Coke from the outside fridge in the shed. You need to be alone. Rodney has made you furious.

"Hi." It is Cassy. You stand there, closer than you might have only days ago. She looks over at the rest of them. They are watching. Everyone knows. "How was the beach?" she says.

The sun lights her long hair from behind. It is like her head is on fire. She's wearing silver earrings. You've never seen them before. She has blue eyes. She has freckles. She has a fine scar above her eyebrow.

"Marco," someone yells out. Splashes follow.

"Wait for us!" you scream out. "Let's get in the pool," you say to Cassy. "I'm hot."

Cool water explodes across your skin and you glide across the bottom like a stingray, staying deep. Rodney screams, "Marco."

Stay deep, work towards the deep end, up for breath, then double back. Keep working this pattern. *World champion bottom skimmer. The man's a legend.* Stomach on cement, you lie very still. You feel an accidental foot hit the small of your back. You surface. It was Rodney's foot.

"You had your eyes open, Rodney." Your accusation is fierce-mouthed.

"Bullcrap. You can't take it," he says.

"Marco?" you say reluctantly. Your eyes close, hands go out feeling, groping.

"Polo!" You hear them sing in chorus and try to imagine the distances between them, guess where they will swim.

The water's thin. You are fast. Everyone's quiet. This is serious Marco Polo again. First proper game all summer.

"Fish out of water?" you scream suddenly. There are squeals. Your toe nicks somebody.

"Got someone!" you yell, opening your eyes.

"It's Cassy. She's on the bottom," says Rodney, creeping across the shallow end with a Coke in his hand. He's out of the pool. Bloody cheater.

"She musta felt it. My foot really whacked her." You lie. It was more like a shave. But this is real again. "Why's she not coming up?" you say, frustrated.

"Go down and get her," says Rodney. "You can kiss under there." Everyone laughs.

You dip under, your arms go up and you sink down. You swim to her. Her floating red hair. Grab her foot and shake and grunt. She just stays there. Controlled panic. You pull her towards yourself. She's stuck. You pull harder. It's like a dream. You move around in front of her. Long hair tangled everywhere.

"She's caught. Her hair. It's in the filter." You go back under, without a big enough mouthful of air; Rodney's there too. He works at her hair. A big noise, then silence — the filter is turned off. She's free. You carry her up in your arms.

Breathing checks. Her red hair, blue eyes, silver earrings, blue lips.

"No pulse," says Rodney.

"You do the compressions. I'll breathe," you tell him and you watch him landmark on her chest. Like you do at the beach every Sunday morning at Junior Surf Life Saving. And you pinch her nose, grab her chin, and blow, and blow. *One one-thousand … two one-thousand.* You find a rhythm. Rodney is crying. Your mother is running and screaming now. Some of the gang steps back. Cassy's red hair is steaming on the hot bricks. You give your breaths and stare at the fine scar above her eyebrow. You are trying to make her live, but already know she will not leave you — that this will never end.

THE PRICE

OF FISH

BELINDA GAVE A TUG on her end of the fishing line and discovered a sluggish weight. In her left hand she gripped a fat roll of coarse-grained cork. Her right hand unwound the line from the cork roll and fed the slack into the ocean. Her eyes climbed the clouds into open sky, seeking out the seagull that squawked above. She gave the line another tug, and again felt the resistance. Maybe it was a rock cod. More likely seaweed, she thought — a great green clump of Neptune's pearls.

"Got something?" Belinda's mother asked.

"Nothing. A snag."

Belinda wound her line in a little. She watched the beads of saltwater clinging to the nylon. Winding, casting: these repetitions relaxed Belinda's mind.

"I'm glad you came, Belinda. Especially this year."

Belinda nodded, acknowledging her mother, but she remained face-out to the sea. Last year, where was she? She was in Vancouver with Jeff. The year before she'd been somewhere else. The Tonga holiday. Jeff had been ill: gastritis.

What should I give him, Mum? Belinda remembered sitting on a wicker chair in their hotel room in Tonga, talking to her mother. As she'd sat there in paradise, she could picture her mother's house, where the woman stood, the colour of the room, the old wood wireless.

Don't fish by yourself, Mum, was what she'd said right before hanging up the phone.

Last year this time, she and Jeff had stayed on in Vancouver for a short holiday — after Jeff attended the conference. It was October, her first North American *fall*. Jeff had prepared her for the season.

"The weather there feels like a fight," he'd said. "One side is wet; the other side is dry. It's so much more dramatic than Sydney."

She'd felt this tension swell as she explored West 4th and Granville Island while Jeff sat in hotel conference rooms. *Crisp* entered her vocabulary. Leaves turned ruddy and rust coloured. Her cheeks went colder the more she explored. To warm them, she ducked inside cafés for piping hot tea. The wool of her cardigan felt wet and warm as she took it all in, loving its absolute newness.

Today, as she cast out her line, she remembered how Jeff had loved the action back at the company's head office.

There are so many more zeros, he'd exclaimed, as if lollies. Jeff called them candies. And *zero* too — another one of Jeff's Canadian words. Sounds perkier than a boring *nought*. Jeff had been on a high when he too felt the wet, then the dry. That, and being back in his hometown, Vancouver. She'd loved how they walked everywhere, sucking in the cool air. On a day trip up a mountain she'd tasted snow for the first time. They stroked wet mossy trees that disappeared up into the clouds like giants, bark that felt like nothing on this earth. They bought new white sweaters, wore thick socks, drank big coffees with cream, ate waffles with syrup. She licked her cracked upper lip. Sea salt.

Now, this year, again with her mother at her side, the Pacific Ocean opened up in front of Belinda like a moat. Her mother's bare legs stood beside her, criss-crossed with purple veins, squiggles, ladder rungs, snakes. Her mother's grey hair was cut straight across, just above shoulder length. Her bob had not changed, but her face had grown more creased, mostly around her eyes. In recent years, in her own isolated imagination, Belinda had drawn her mother's face placid, like the sea from an aircraft window. Now up close, her mother's real face had stormy complexities, irregularities. There was a curl in her smile and a new wave in her hair. Is this what Belinda herself would look like in later years?

"I didn't tell you," her mother began, "your cousin Bernard almost made it today. But he's got an exam."

It was Bernard, as a boy, who, almost twenty years ago, had inadvertently started these annual fishing excursions on the anniversary of Belinda's father's death. Belinda wound her line once more around the cork, taking up the excess slack. She could almost hear Bernard's voice.

"My dad said I could go fishing. Take us to the beach, Aunty Bernice." On and on, the ten-year-old boy had whined.

Belinda pictured Bernard, not as he was now, but as he was at ten: tough, scabbed elbows and knees — the consequence of growing up on a sheep property northwest of Moree. Belinda's uncle had sent him to the city to stay with them for a week that summer.

"Of course he should come!" Belinda's mother had said to her brother on the phone. "He'll take our minds off the date. He'll be no trouble."

At the time, Belinda's mother had admitted to her, "If your father were alive, he'd have taken Bernard fishing. It would have been a 'boys only' day."

But Belinda's mother decided to make the best of things and turned the day into a game: they were to be pirates.

First, they had to catch their food and then, in the afternoon, they'd search for treasure. In the garage, Peg-leg, Blackbeard, and Belinda found some booty: fishing line, corks, tackle, a rusty fish descaler, sinkers, floats, and a knife. From the corner shop they acquired a bag of frozen bloodworms.

Standing on the very same rock shelf, looking out over the same stretch of Pacific Ocean, it took little effort for Belinda to reconstruct that first fishing trip. Her mother had packed a light picnic all those years ago and she had done the same today, right down to the same old silver thermos.

"Don't touch anything blue," Belinda's mother had warned Bernard when he ventured down into a rock pool. "Might be a blue-ringed octopus. They'll kill a young pirate in a minute." Belinda watched Bernard looking about him in the rock pool: seeing nothing blue, he grew doubtful such things existed, and chased and hunted tiny crabs. Belinda and her mother stood side by side and fished for hours. Belinda had felt grown up that day, next to her mother.

The following anniversary, mother and daughter remembered what they'd done last year to see the day out. Recollections of tangled lines, worms, and sandy sandwiches brought back strangely pleasant memories. They went again, this time without Bernard.

Until Belinda left home and moved in with Jeff, *Jeff the Canadian*, which often meant leaving Australia for months at a time, for all those years, the two of them — mother and daughter — fished that anniversary morning away. Years of casting, winding, fishing. Now this.

She looked over at her mother.

"I'm moving to Canada, to Vancouver, Mum."

There. She'd said it. Jeff worked for a forestry company. The promotion he'd been after meant the company's head office. She explained this to her mother.

"Are you going to be married now?"

Her mother did not look at her as she said this; rather, her attention was fixed on threading the bloodworm onto the hook held between her index finger and thumb.

Belinda ignored the question and wound her line once around the cork roll. She looked down at her feet. Last night she'd painted her toenails red. The rock shelf they fished from consisted of sedimentary layers, tan and orange and white. Belinda kicked off her sandals and felt the warm sandstone. She glanced up and saw the sails of a boat on the horizon. Then a beach helicopter — on the lookout for lone, stranded swimmers or schools of sharks — scoured the middle distance. Belinda noticed a seagull hovering, only just out of arm's reach, waiting to see what she had on the end of her line. Perhaps there would be leftovers, guts, scraps.

Still winding, Belinda walked forward and stepped into a shallow rock pool by the water's edge. The trapped water, abandoned by last night's high tide, was warm. In the ankle-deep pool, sea anemone fished for food with their fleshy tentacles and soft-sucking centres, a crab the size of a one-cent piece scuttled off into a hidden groove, and the crushed shells and sand carpeting the rock pool floor swelled up in angry storm clouds each time Belinda moved, shuffled her feet, wiggled her painted toes.

A great scribble of seaweed, fishing line, tackle, and blood-worm rose to the surface about ten metres out. Belinda pulled the mass towards her, lifting it up out of the water.

"Should I cut it and put a new hook on?"

"Are you sure you can't save it?" her mother said.

Her mother saved everything. Belinda had seen a snippet of her own baby hair, her first nail clippings, and she understood that the small brown dried-up worm in a plastic bag was a petrified portion of her own umbilical cord. Belinda's mother had also saved all Belinda's clothes from her childhood years in green garbage bags out in the garage, her first Tony Roche Special tennis racket, and every painting Belinda had ever made at school. Her mother's photograph albums were numbered, with dates and names of persons scratched in the margins. Towards the back of the upright freezer in the garage, was a double-bagged Tupperware container, the contents of which had come up only last year during a spring cleaning.

"Mum, what's in this one?" Belinda had asked, with the lid open, lightly sniffing.

"A wedge of my thirty-one-year-old wedding cake [laugh-ter]. It sure outlasted the groom."

"I can't believe you just said that."

Now, Belinda took a knife and cut at the seaweed, tossing scraps back into the sea. At the core was a tight ball of fishing line wrapped around its own sinker and hook. She picked at it for a moment.

"You always get snags."

The seagull squawked and flew off with an empty beak.

It was almost lunch. They collected up their fishing tackle,

THE PRICE OF FISH ■ 105

thermos, and towel and walked back through the park to the car. For Belinda the smell of the old VW — car oil, sunscreen, lanolin, banana peel — reminded her of her childhood. She remembered her father's big hairy legs tucked under the wheel and his hand on the stick, changing gears as he sang along with the AM radio he'd installed himself. The seats had always been hot and sticky. She scratched at the sea salt itching her scalp and rolled down the window, taking in the beginnings of summer happening around her.

Everything was familiar. It seemed to her that nothing had changed in all the years she'd been gone. Her mother still frequented the same butcher, had her hair cut by the same stylist, enjoyed the same friends. Her conversation had changed little in content, if at all.

Belinda had planned to stay the night and drive back into the city tomorrow. She'd go to The Workers Club with her mother for roast lamb and force down the junket for dessert. Her mother would play the poker machines with Mrs. Ritchie and her Aunt Sally. She'd sit quietly at a table in the corner, read a book, nurse a beer.

This dinner outing was a predictable event whenever she came home — Christmas, the anniversary of her father's passing, her mother's birthday. She thought about these things as the old VW wound its way back to her mother's house.

Aunt Sally was coming over for tea at four. They'd go to the club in her car. Belinda's mother went for a nap and left Belinda in the sunroom with the *Sydney Morning Herald* and a cup of tea. She looked around: a black porcelain leopard with green jewelled eyes; the upright piano; the blue tartan fabric on the chairs; the rug, a series of concentric circles culminating in a dot. Belinda was intimate even with the bricks, the misshapen ones, and the room's curves, the corners, the light fixtures. All were familiar; the inescapable effort of remembering the times and people associated with each of them, exhausting.

Aunt Sally arrived an hour early with a great cascade of kisses and hugs, tarts, biscuits, and questions. She apologized for being early: *No, no, don't wake your mother, us girls'll just have a chat out on the verandah.* And Belinda brewed more tea and sat with Aunt Sally — she was the local high school principal — and got caught up on the lives and misfortunes of her classmates from public high school, none of whom, it seemed, had ever left the shire.

The three women met Mrs. Ritchie, Belinda's mother's oldest friend, at The Workers Club at six-thirty. They stood in line and were served lamb roast, peas, and sweet potato, all drowning in gravy. Today, mercifully, there was custard instead of junket.

"Catch any fish today?" asked Mrs. Ritchie. They hadn't, of course, but Belinda's mother did tell the story of Belinda's long struggle with the seaweed in an exaggerated, one-that-got-away style.

"Well, we're glad you came this year, for your mother," said Mrs. Ritchie. "It's twenty years today since Harold died. Isn't that what you told us last week, Bernice?"

Belinda's mother nodded, but only slightly.

"Oh, Mum. Twenty years *exactly*? I didn't realize. I'm sorry."

"I'd managed to keep it out of mind myself. Until just now, dear." Belinda's mother gave Mrs. Ritchie a look so hard that it could have bored holes through her best friend.

"So what's new with you, Belinda?" said Mrs. Ritchie, so obviously trying to change the topic that Aunt Sally laughed a little.

"Nothing, really," said Belinda. There was another moment of silence. Belinda waited to see if her mother would announce her plans for Vancouver.

After dinner the three older women left Belinda to her book and bought rolls of twenty-cent pieces and headed over to the poker machines. Belinda found it difficult to concentrate on the page and so she looked around the long room. The orange and black carpet continued up the walls for about a metre. The ceiling, originally white, now yellow from years of smoke, was covered in pointy stucco. She was the youngest person in the place by an even generation. Twenty years, she thought. Her father, gone, twenty years.

With the horse races broadcast over the television and old war veterans and mates from the union gathered round tables telling stories and buying rounds, Belinda felt invisible. She sat like this, unnoticed, for about an hour, sipping a beer, reading now and then from her novel, but mostly just watching. Her mother, Aunty Sally, and Mrs. Ritchie left after a time, but she stayed to finish her drink. Anything to delay going back to the house.

Her own bed felt smaller than she'd remembered it. The sheets were damp; they must have come straight off the line. The night was humid, dark, and close. Cicadas started up periodically. The neighbour's dog barked, chasing ghosts all night. Poor deaf thing, Belinda thought.

Belinda slept among fragmented dreams. Her father had spoken to her. His big, even sentences, his pipe breath. He took her to the library where they looked up famous people for projects she was doing for school: William Dampier, Helen Keller, Douglas Bader, James Cook, Florence Nightingale.

Next, she was at a friend's funeral: the girl from next door who had died so many years ago now. She'd drowned in a backyard swimming pool, her hair caught in the filter. Belinda saw the hard wooden church pew in front of her. The day was so hot her dress stuck to her back. The boys had snickered in front of her, behind her, swirling faces, the girl's white face in the casket looking up at the roof, the yellow stucco roof, men drinking beer, pouring it out of jugs into glasses, beer into glasses, Jeff's strong arms holding her, her mother pouring tea by the sea, storm clouds of sand around her whole body running, slipping, into a shallow groove of mossy bark, escaping all movement, all around her, her, her, her mother shook her.

"Tea? Belinda, want tea?" Belinda, covered in a cool sweat, looked up at her mother leaning over the bed. It was a moment before Belinda realized that she was naked in front of her mother, and that this was not the usual set of circumstances to which she awoke. She moved her arm out and it touched not Jeff but the wall. She was at home.

ON THE VERANDAH, Belinda and her mother ate poached eggs on toast and drank tea. After breakfast Belinda gathered together her things and walked them out to the car.

"I'll see you soon, Mum. Thanks."

Her mother patted her cheek twice in the same soft manner she'd always done. It was her way.

Belinda climbed into her car and began the trip back into the centre of Sydney. The drive was a fair distance, three-quarters of an hour or so. Perhaps she'd stop at the university and have a short visit with her cousin Bernard.

In a traffic jam on the Tom Ugly's Bridge, the December heat dazzled and danced about on the bonnet of her car. Belinda glanced down at her red toes. Vancouver, Vancouver. Then, in the shimmering waves, the word *crisp* came to her, a hook too luring not to bite.

ABOUT
WALKING

D EVLIN RESTS OUTSIDE the shoe store on a bench, three shopping bags propped between his tired feet. He observes his sister, Sue, or more correctly Sue's head, how it bobs between aisles, dipping for a moment below his line of sight, then resurfacing as she scours the racks of shoes before her. He imagines that she will turn this into a lesson for her pupils. A class full of new Australians, Sue will coax them to say the words aloud together. Straps. Heels. Buckles. Bows. Bride. She is after just the right pair for walking down the aisle.

Above Devlin, the cathedral-style roof soars in ribbed, steel arches and sheets of glass the size of whole swimming pools. Higher up still, an office tower looks as if it is swaying in the wind. The sky is blue and natural light floods the shopping complex, giving the illusion that this inside is, in fact, out of doors. About him shoppers drift past with determined looks, clutching at great buys, and children. Beside the shoe store there is a food counter. Sue, gesturing to the clerk who is gathering more shoes for her to try on, remains completely engrossed. Devlin takes this moment to step over and order a hotdog from the man behind the food counter.

"Mustard, please. Lots of mustard," says Devlin.

Warm, white bun, soft, and the taste of the mustard. He is a mustard lover. Hotter the mustard the better. He sits down once more — bags, bench, cathedral ceiling — and he eats. He wonders why his sister, who is to be married on Friday, forgot to try on shoes until now. Even he knows this is too last-minute for a bride-to-be. Sue is usually so organized; he loves that about her. Devlin can see that she is telling the clerk about why the shoes must be perfect. She beams uncontrollably. Everything will be perfect. Her happiness, living inside this moment, is complete and unquestionable.

The body falls from the sky accompanied by a spray of glass shards and a single, baritone scream. It strikes the ground outside the shoe store, dividing the distance equally between Devlin and his sister. The impact of the body is such that it brakes the tiling on the floor — where it hits, the epicentre, forks of force shoot off like lightning, splitting the grout in all directions. The sound of it: a sickening, dull wallop. Blue oxford dress shirt. Khaki pants, creased. Brown belt and shoes. The man's body bounces once, unnaturally, like a dropped bowling ball, but remains remarkably intact. Only the head, skull dashed, face stuck to the tiling preserving his last expression inside out, is unrecognisable as that of a human.

Devlin will spend the next days trying to free his mouth from the taste of mustard.

THE PATH MEANDERS BETWEEN smooth sandstone and light scrub, a gentle hill, downwards. Three days after the body fell from the sky, and just two days before the wedding, Devlin turns to catch the glint of copper windchimes hanging sound-less from the back verandah. The still, still of the morning. Yet, he hears the chimes. In his mind they echo from last night, family friends laughing, barbecuing sausages, the cricket on the radio, someone's child singing in rhyme, splashing from the wading pool that Devlin himself had filled with the old hose.

Devlin walks away down the hill from his backyard. This is the edge of Sydney. His verandah — the overhang with its leaf-clogged gutter, the weary floorboards, the Australian wilderness picture-framed by vertical posts — is among the very last licks of this part of Sydney's sprawl. After it, there is nothing but blue haze, eucalypts, and heat waves for weeks. As he walks, around him is sudden noise. Bird calls. Then, just as suddenly, their lull, sonic endlessness. This is a country of edges and, for six years now, Devlin and Sue have lived on one of its precipices.

Devlin bought the land seven years ago. Contracted an architect, a builder, a landscaper — the lot. Moved in by himself. His castle. Then, soon after, his youngest sister, Sue, came to live with him. Initially, Sue had just needed somewhere to stay temporarily, while she looked for a place of her own in the city. But time passed and she stayed on. Devlin didn't mind. He was almost twenty years older than she. He'd been long gone from his parents' house by the time she was a girl taking ballet lessons, skipping through the sprinkler on hot days. So, when Sue moved in they got to know one another, and Devlin liked what he found.

They were "roommates," as Sue liked to refer to their living arrangement. During these six years she first attended university, then found a job teaching English to new Australian immigrants in the city. At the English school, she met another teacher, a nice bloke, Gavin. Gavin and Sue started to see each other frequently. Devlin approved of this Gavin and so when he began to sleep over once in a while, Devlin got used to the sight of him first thing in the morning. They all got along famously.

As Devlin walks, he thinks once again about the afternoon six months ago when he opened his door in response to a lively knock. There was Sue and Gavin standing there, both with big grins on their faces.

"Why didn't you use your key, Sue?" he'd said. The grins dissipated into tears of joy, hugs, backslaps of congratulation, a lot of head shaking in disbelief, in the wonderful surprise of it all. They were to be married. They erupted into retellings of the proposal, the beach, and the sunlight. What he'd said. How she'd answered. That she suspected something was up but wasn't sure. That choosing the ring had been the most difficult thing he'd ever had to do.

Devlin descends farther along the path winding into the overgrown valley below. He walks slowly, choosing his steps carefully. His mind is alive with details, so many details. In the months that followed the proposal, dates were set and a church booked. Devlin was to take care of the food. Invitations were sent to family and friends, near and far. Soon the day had drawn close. Last-minute particulars included gifts for the groom, and somehow, Sue, poor Sue announced to him in tears, that she had forgotten to buy shoes.

"I'll take you to the shops tomorrow," he'd said with a reassuring firmness. And they did go shopping, but after several hours they had still not found *just the right pair*. Outside yet another shoe store he'd bought a hot dog, tasted mustard and, with its thunderclap and lightning strike, the body had fallen between them.

"Should the wedding be postponed?" There. Yesterday, Devlin had finally said what was on all their minds. It was three days before the wedding, two days after the body had fallen from the sky and into their lives. Devlin, Sue, Gavin, and both sets of parents were at Devlin's kitchen table. Sue was beside herself. She did not want the day to be ruined. No one wanted to be disrespectful to the fallen man, who as it turns out did not jump in an act of suicide, but was simply leaning against the window in his office high above when it popped out, he right along with it. A tragic accident.

In the end, they decided to go ahead with the wedding. This decision was arrived at primarily because Sue had only *heard* the impact and did not, thanks to the astonishingly fast-thinking sales clerk, actually *see* the body. While hearing it was generally agreed to be bad enough, so much had been organized, put in place, spent, that to undo it all now would make it, almost, worse. The show was to go on.

Devlin's sandals are new and hurting his feet. It is still morning, but it is hot and he can feel the heat beginning to swell in the bush about him. The track, one Devlin has wandered many times, winds down from the foot of his backyard all the way to the creek. At the creek there is a clearing. If, like most visitors, you come to it from the main road by car, you can bring baskets of food and drink, radios and badminton nets, and sit at one of the public picnic tables and eat the chicken sandwiches that you made and wrapped yourself. This is precisely the plan already in place for the day following the wedding — something easy and familiar. Everyone will gather down at the clearing, have a picnic, and relax after the big day. Then that evening, Sue and Gavin will depart on their honeymoon to Noosa.

Devlin finds the picnic area empty of people. It is too early for fun. This is what he had hoped. He wants to be alone. He passes through the dappled shade, past the clusters of rubbish bins, overflowing, chained together, fetid, and interrupts a possum vulturing a chicken carcass. Licking the inside of the foil bag, the possum stops, sensing Devlin's presence, and looks up at him.

On the other side of the picnic area a path leads off on a five-kilometre bush walk. Difficulty level: easy. "Follow green markers. Stay on path." These are the instructions on the brown sign with yellow writing that sports the insignia of the National Parks and Wildlife Service. Devlin decides to further stretch his legs.

Again, all day yesterday morning, he couldn't shake the dull thumping sound of the body bouncing off the ground. Glass, and bits of bone, and brain, and blood, had showered him, slapping against his face, matting in his hair. And all he could taste was mustard. Then, at noon, the meeting at his kitchen table. He had not wanted to add an extra burden to the situation, to Sue and Gavin, by revealing his state of mind. That they were to proceed with the wedding was their decision. But privately he'd hoped for the opposite outcome. Sue needed some time here, he'd thought. It was their future happiness at stake, after all. He'd decided to go into the office to clear his mind. Numbers, flow charts, anything to distract him, even for a few hours. Although he only worked on the fifth floor, he found himself standing by a window looking down. At the photocopier, a co-worker had asked him how he was. He'd mumbled through. He was most concerned about Sue, he'd said.

Devlin passes a green marker. The sign says he has journeyed one kilometre. Around him the bush is alive. Cicadas and birds, trees smelling of hot eucalypt. He sees a stream at the bottom of a long, densely treed slope. It takes him, draws him in, this stream does, inducing a feeling of calm. It is so welcoming that Devlin leaves the path and makes his way down the embankment to the creek below.

Up close, the creek is thin and improbable. It winds its way along a sandy-bottomed vein that is the eventual drain for rain runoff or seepage. Devlin takes his sandals off. He stands barefoot in the creek on a rock. There is a blister on his ankle and the cool water on his feet feels good.

Suddenly, he becomes aware of the silence. Then there is a loud booming rush in the bush to his right. Devlin's heart leaps, he squats low. He can't yet see what is crashing through the bush, branches cracking as it descends towards him. It is closer, louder, coming closer and getting louder; he wants to run but cannot; the noise of it increases further, louder, faster. But it does not strike; instead it remains out of sight.

It is almost midday now. Devlin makes his way along the other side of the ravine hoping to outfox whatever it was that decided, at the last second, not to attack. He scampers, grabs at rocks and tree roots, trying to get higher on the ravine. It is following him, he is sure of it. He tells himself he is making good time, good progress, and after some climbing he comes to a small cliff face. Using cracks and grooves, he scales it, hauling his body up, at last, on top of the ridge. From here he can see where he is; he is in the middle of nowhere. Blue, hazy stillness for kilometres. He talks to himself as he surveys all of this nothing. The words come slowly at first, then fluidly.

"Sue's at the blackboard. Lists of words in columns. Simple ones. Book, tent, fork, left, bike. Those with some experience, more difficult words. Pamphlet, structure, utensil, direction, scooter.

I help her think of them sometimes. Not to teach them what these words mean. Only help these foreigners say the words. Another teacher's job, Gavin's maybe, maybe Gavin's, to work on meaning. He'll be something like: Go to the greengrocer's and buy food. 'May I have four potatoes?' they say together. Or to the butcher's. 'Six lamb chops and four sausages, please.'"

The sun beats down. Devlin is shivering. He starts moving down the side of the ravine, rock by rock, some of which fall down ahead of him, showing him the way.

"Scenarios versus oral classes is a new method. Sue's idea, if I have it right, is that even if pupils do not know what these words mean, they've got to spend time pronouncing as many sounds in English as possible. Makes them less intimidated. To learn new words. Along with what they mean. You know, later on.

"Day after day, she helps them. Mandarin people pronounce thicket, biscuit, and wicket. Arabic people to say dollop, Collie, and flotsam. These twenty of them sometimes. How to form the shape to make these sounds. New words. For the first time. I'll be stuffed. Couldn't do it myself."

Devlin is bleeding from a cut above his eye. "Bloody blood. How'd I ding my head?" Flies collect about him, landing and departing, drawn to his sweat and now his blood. The day beats down, wave after wave of heat. The bush goes on around his chattering. It is oblivious, unmoved, inhuman.

"Last Christmas we hosted a graduation party down at the clearing. All these immigrants from places like Turkey, China and Chile. Mate, I watched Sue and Gavin as they doled out the food that the guests had brought — sharing a bit of their homelands with their class members. It was then Sue gave her final piece of advice, 'Make your children practice with you; they will learn faster than you and can help you.' Sue's been at this for a long time now. Almost as long as she's been with me. Yeah. The end of each year, her students never want to be finished. They don't want her to go. They kind of cling to her in desperate little groups. Try to memorize her every word. Just being here in Australia with Sue is a dream come true. And now they are saying these impossible English words, too. They are hoping it will all not end when Sue leaves them."

For a while Devlin had felt hungry, but now he is thirsty. He does not have a watch, and he has become oblivious to the day around him. It is late afternoon and he has been walking for hours. The blister on his ankle is also bleeding, but it no longer gives him pain. He tries to keep the flies off it, swatting at it with his other foot as he walks, stumbling along.

"Although I don't care for the cheese itself, you gotta love the word Gorgonzola. Bloody spectacular word. Gothic, mate. Transylvanian sounding. Read Dracula as a boy under the sheets with my torch. Very scary, at the time. Remember the feel of the sheets on me bed. The house I grew up in. The bedroom that I shared with my brother, Henry. Should have spoken to Henry about the wedding? God, the wedding, I'll miss the bloody wedding. Shit, mate. Mate. Mate, oh, mate."

In the night the bush unfolds in pockets of phantom light and darkness. Devlin leans against a tree, but eventually slides down to the ground. Wind shakes the branches and they dance above him. Twice already, he has heard the crashing sound. It comes closer and closer, drawing speed and increasing in volume. Then it vanishes.

He dreams he is sailing on a boat with big white sails, that he is in a bed with white sheets. He hears the sound of wind chimes. He is eating pakoras, chimichungas, dim sum. He swims down straight lanes in butterfly strokes and a crowd cheers him on. He rides a camel in a desert, plays a phonograph and shakes the hands of fashionable Jazz age characters at a summer wedding. He floats in the air, holding onto a balloon, not holding the balloon, the ground skipping below him, not there at all but open ocean. He eats hotdogs, the mustard stifling, mustard gas, choking him, colleagues from work laugh at him. His sister speaks, "Do you know why I am doing this to you?" Devlin answers her, but his words are not able to be heard, the mustard has burned his voice away. He tries to shout. Nothing comes from his mouth at first, then it bursts open in a geyser of hateful words and blood. Her head is dashed.

He is speechless, silent, dumbstruck. Sue is alive again. She cuts chops and sausages on a board into cubes. She eats the meat raw, takes his hand and they go into a valley together and swim in a wading pool.

"We drink the water between our legs," he hears himself say. They are younger. Children. It is daylight.

"SIERRA WHISKEY ALPHA. Section three sweep complete. Over."

"Thank you, Alpha. Over."

The authorities are positive Devlin is in the bush now. When he did not return last night, the police handed over the case to the national park search and rescue team. The worry was, and still is, that the bush surrounding their house is dense, the ravines are steep. The risk is that he's had a fall.

They begin tracking with two dogs. Fixing on the scent of the shirt he wore yesterday, the dogs immediately tear off the verandah and down the back path. By the time the dogs find the spot where he left the track, it is too late, too dark to continue with the search. It will have to wait for the morning. So plans are made. Fifteen men will assemble at 5:30 a.m. tomorrow morning, by the picnic tables. There will be more dogs, walkie-talkies, and a helicopter brought in — if they've not found him by lunchtime.

Sue calls off the wedding. She is given something to sleep. Gavin watches her breathe, the entire night.

THE BUSH THICKENS AROUND DEVLIN. He is crawling, brushing off ants, pulling himself up inclines, tripping, resting on fallen branches. Out of hunger, he eats a plant. He throws up. It comes green and sour from the depths of him, at first. Then in a second wave: full, hard, bloody. *The last of the mustard.* He makes it to the top of a ravine. In the blue distance he believes he sees the sea. *I am halfway there.*

He makes his way down to the bottom of a gully. The air is cooler and the trees form a canopy over his head, keeping in the sweet air, full of ripe hotness. He travels along the gully where the trees are close together. Rock faces grow and become steeper on either side. They narrow, but do not close up completely. They rise. On either side of him. Vertical slabs rise into the sky.

I am a pilgrim. Others will follow on my route. Like Santiago de Compostella. Gorgonzola. I sing the words of the foreigners.

I accompany myself on my way. I find a cave. Blown into the sandstone by the wind. It is not deep; I climb up to it. I look out to the bush as if I am on my verandah. The tree branches are so high above.

He sees thin lines of white ants emerge from a tiny hole. The moon comes out. Shapes and shadows form in the gully below, the sway of trees, the glint of moonlight off white bark and leaves that rush in the wind. *I hear a kookaburra. When I sleep, I do so deeply. I remember nothing.*

"Sue! Sue."

A snake has bitten me. I do not know my varieties. I may die now. I've ripped it from my leg and thrown it from the cave. Perhaps it was not poisonous at all. I sit in a stillness as if praying in a cathedral. I am drunk. Now angry. Embarrassed. This all passes before the reason I feel it can take hold. I count myself down. I breathe five shallow breaths. One. I may die in a matter of hours. Two. In a matter of minutes. Three. The clouds are white above the clifftop and the sun casts no shadow of me. Four. There are tears. Hot, wet tears. I am laughing.

He beams, uncontrollably. Everything will be perfect.

THE SLOW
WAR CRY OF
GRAMMAR

REGIMENTAL SERGEANT MAJOR Irish, tall, muscular, had not seen his naked feet for two weeks. His boots were laced tight before first light and wrenched off well after dark. The balls of his feet had not felt the hot rock and creek beds they'd crossed. His toes had not winced when they kicked an old burnt stump down by the track's end. His soft, white feet had gone spared, indirectly, from feeling.

This morning RSM Irish placed his Dixie pan full of gritty instant coffee down at his side on the damp earth. Then, as he rolled his first cigarette, once more he was unsurprised to see young Hacket copying his ways. Carefully. Right down to the swift taps of his cigarette on the back of his lighter. The other ten cadets, scattered about under ground sheets, in sleeping bags, slept on.

Around the boys' campfire there was just bush, bush sounds and birds that continued on for three days' march. If you'd chanced to head in the right direction, you'd come to a small town nestled in the southern highlands of New South Wales. If not, just bush, birds, the odd fly, bugger all else.

Flat light and dew blurred the edges of the eucalyptus leaves up high. There'll be no sun today, thought Irish, peering skyward.

"RSM Irish?"

"What, Hacket?" he said, spitting a piece of tobacco off the end of his tongue.

"Last day t'morra."

"Yeah, mate. Bloody 'strewth. Not soon enough." Irish looked at Hacket in the eyes. "Any longer out here and you yourself would have been a choice."

The platoon had marched fourteen kilometres yesterday on the back of eighteen the day before. The long and brutal march out was a tradition at Australian Grammar, their huge and insular military boarding school. Irish dropped his eyes from Hacket, letting him off. The boy looked exhausted. He was only thirteen years old. Year eight. Tiny, thin legs. Might as well be on a girl, Irish reckoned when he'd first laid eyes on him. How's he gunna lift that pack? Soon, though, Irish figured he might turn into a good little bloke. Top bloke, even though he's a day boy, from the city, from Vaucluse, whatever the hell that is. But, he seems loyal. Maybe he'll make a good corporal … next year.

Next year, thought Irish. When he'd be done with high school and after the HSC exams were all over. You can't really think past 'em, though. They're like a wall around a bloke's mind. Irish felt the whiskers on his chin. After two weeks on bivouac they might be the longest they'd ever grown. His chin was only four years older than Hacket's.

About them the morning was damp but the bush had seen no real rain. The wood was dry. The creek bed they'd followed for two days, dry. The air after sunrise, dry. That's why the sound of a thick branch snapping, something the size of an arm or a leg, echoed for what seemed like a whole minute.

"Guess we'd better …" said Irish. He surveyed the camp. A few heads of the sleeping cadets rose. They looked over at Irish to make sure all was right, then wilted back onto their rolled, ripe towels which acted as pillows. Irish tied his boots and walked in the direction of the noise. Hacket trailed a few steps behind, coughing a little on his cigarette.

They walked through the bush, away from the camp in a wide arc. Irish had reckoned almost immediately it was just a branch breaking, but he decided to stretch his legs a little, have some quiet before the day. He was thinking about his father as he walked. The way the man's fist had felt when Irish was a small boy and he'd swung from it on the back verandah. Both hands clasped around it, his arms outstretched. His father laughing, holding out his thick arm like a tree branch for his small son to play on. *Down you get, mate,* the old man would say, when the game was over, his huge arm finally tiring. That'd been when they still lived in Dubbo. Now they were on a property near Walgett. Sheep and wheat, mainly. When there was rain. Didn't see why his father was making him go to Uni next year, only to have to come back to that.

"Do ya think it's this way?" asked Hacket.

"What?" said Irish, annoyed that the boy'd spoken.

"What made the noise?"

"I dunno. We're just walking. Why don't you rack-off back?"

All of a sudden Irish pulled up as a sharp jab, a rock caught in his boot, sunk into his heel. He hobbled for a second, then sat down and began to undo his laces. Hacket just watched.

"What are *you* looking at?" said Irish.

"What's wrong?"

"Nothing. I just got a rock. No, you know what, you are," said Irish, without thinking, but glad he did. "You're what's wrong. Everywhere I go, you're there. I can't even have a minute to …" but he stopped, looking at Hacket. He didn't take his eyes from him as he up-ended his boot and felt the small stone fall from inside. He rubbed his socked foot. Then ripped it off and looked at the sole of his bare heel. The pebble had not punctured the skin, but the sight of his own pale, damp foot startled him a little. His own body, his skin, seemed so foreign.

"Take your boots off, Hacket," said Irish in a tone Hacket had never heard before. Hacket's small, delicate face creased at the command somewhat, but he acquiesced, falling to the ground and removing his boots and his socks as well, the last part without being asked.

"Would you do whatever I told you to do?" asked Irish. The silence of the bush around them hung expectant.

Hacket did not respond. Irish knew that he sensed this was getting serious, and that he must not have known what he did to bring it on.

To Irish, tears seemed to well in the boy's eyes as the lad realized where this was headed. But Irish knew he had to do it at least once. Go through with it. His exams were coming and it would all be over soon.

"Show me the respect of Grammar, Cadet," said Irish.

Somewhere a currawong let out a cry that filled the bush with ease and made all, to Irish, seem familiar. A sound at home, in the right place, just being its ordinary self.

"Please, RSM Irish," was all Hacket uttered, softly. Real tears welled now, rolling down his cheeks. He wanted to be back at school, cramming his Latin and French books into his locker, drawing isosceles triangles and figuring angles on smooth lined foolscap, watching teachers perform experiments over Bunsen burners — their rubber hoses sliding snugly over the gas taps, or writing the definitions for parts of speech on English pop-tests. But he knew better than to protest. And even though this was his first time, he knew what to do. Hacket unfastened his brass belt; the buttons on his khakis fell away out of their eyelets with ease. He pushed his pale brown underwear — the ones with the end-to-end rows of model T Fords on them — to the ground. Irish cupped Hacket's nuts.

"Sing it," said Irish, towering over him, cadet Hacket's clammy, hairless balls — lolling about, then contracting — in his half-clutched fingers, the boy's uncircumcised dick resting on his thick, bare wrist. Irish had trapped Hacket's gaze in his own. There was no defusing this now.

Slightly faster, and higher than it would have been scored, between gasps of air and suppressed sobs, Hacket sang the first verse and chorus of "The Slow War Cry of Grammar." A publicly unsung hymn set to the tune of "Onward! Christian Soldiers," not written down, but known off by heart to every Grammar boy. It was passed down from generation to generation, father to son, brother to brother, mate to mate. Just in case they're ever asked to show an older boy, *the respect of Grammar.*

At the end of the refrain, Irish watched Hacket take a deep breath. The boy's fear was real. Being asked to sing "The Slow War Cry of Grammar" was a mug's game. It was as self-sentencing as Russian roulette. It had everything to do with chance. Get a stiff on, even if it's simply based on fear or the heat from the first touch of a foreign hand, and you were done for — a poofter, a stinger, a Cranbrook boy. The word would spread and you would be beaten to a pulp for sport, for the rest of your high school days.

What made it worse, was that for Hacket, still new to this confined world of Grammar, Irish was a wonder to behold. Irish was manhood realized; he knew the bush, the rules. He had all that Hacket desired to be and become.

So, as Hacket finished singing, he took a mental picture of Irish's expression right before the older boy was to cast his eyes down and proclaim his future. And Hacket, still unsure of the status of his dick, for a split second wondered if he should be brave and not look down at all but rather keep his eyes on Irish, to study his face a little longer, so he might one day be able to adopt such an expression — if fate fell in his favour, and he was allowed a turn of his own.

LIGHT SWEET
CRUDE

L IFE, THOUGHT RILEY, is easy and good. He pulled his tie straight and a smile grew on his face. Easy and good. Then Riley turned to her.

"How do I look?" he asked.

Across from Riley, sat Jack in her kitchen nook on a stool. The flat was not much more than a single, rectangular room with a kitchen at one end. This was suggested primarily by a change in the flooring from carpet to linoleum. The bedroom lay at the other end. In between was where Jack ate her meals, read her mechanic magazines, and watched TV. A compact bathroom was the only separate room in the place.

"Will you come again tonight?" she asked.

Riley shook his head.

"Why not?"

"My wife. She's expecting me home."

Silence followed. Riley took the opportunity to run a comb through his thinning hair, check his look. At least, he thought briefly, he was not fat. No beer gut. Not too bad for almost fifty.

"So. I'll see you," he said, turning back to face Jack. This produced no reaction from her. He raised his eyebrows, which in turn pulled up the corners of his mouth into a slack smile. He did this in the hopes of a dismissal, of being let go. But there was, obviously, something he still needed to say. Either that or he'd just said something entirely wrong. It was the truth; his wife *was* expecting him that evening. When, he had lately begun to wonder, had honesty become something to avoid?

"Thanks," offered Riley. He'd said it as sweetly as he could, with obvious reference to all that she'd given him last night — her long legs, bare breasts, all of it. Yes it was, after all, a kind of gift. She was a bombshell, this one. So firm and young. But, really, he needed to get to work. Why did she continue to simply sit and sip at her cup of tea? If she could just say something dismissive, like, "Fine, then, go." That would do. He wasn't even after something pleasant necessarily — although that would be nice. Truthfully, he just wished to leave.

Riley had met Jack the way he met most of the women with whom he ended up in this position: ostensibly by chance, but with the lurking hint of intention. Jack worked at the garage where Riley took his car to be serviced. They'd talked initially about his dead battery. How could such a new battery be dead already, he'd wanted to know? So they'd talked a little. He'd been attracted to her from the first minute. He'd found himself smiling much too hard.

The next time they met was the following day. He was back at the garage to pick up his car, half scanning the comings and goings of the mechanics in the background to catch a glimpse of her — but it seemed she was not around. So he climbed into his car. As he pulled out of the lot, Jack was pulling in; their view of one another was obstructed by one of the garage's large "End of Model" sale signs.

The crash wasn't terrible, the screech of tires short-lived. Neither was hurt. Pieces of taillight and fender were scattered about, the smell of rubber lingered in the air.

"I'm so sorry," Jack had said. "God, I'm gunna lose my job."

"You're not going to lose your job."

"Shit. Shit. Shit," she said, scrunching up her face.

Riley placed his hand on Jack's shoulder, to comfort her. He did this out of instinct, mostly. The owner of the garage was on the scene quick smart, about to tear his employee to pieces in front of a loyal, rich customer, when Riley stopped him short.

"It was all my fault," said Riley, manufacturing a kind of gallantry from thin air. "I wasn't paying attention. I'll cover the damage to both."

On the surface, he'd been very decent, selfless. She'd been made to notice him — that was certain. Nonetheless, Riley was still surprised when Jack later telephoned and asked if she could buy him a drink — to thank him for being so good about it all, were her words.

They met at The Workers Club. He'd never actually been inside the place. It hadn't occurred to him that half the blokes who worked for him would be sitting around the bar, drinking, watching the horses. They didn't seem to mind his presence. Perhaps it was because he was there with this young woman. Perhaps, with such stunning company, there are some things that can be overlooked, even the distaste employees likely feel for a boss. Whatever the reason, Jack and Riley were left to themselves as they hunched together around the corner table.

"Jack. That's a funny name for a girl, isn't it?"

"No," she said, smiling, looking up at him, and tucking a strand of blonde hair in behind her ear.

She came on to him with a swiftness he'd not before experienced. Jack was clear from the beginning. She wanted him.

And badly. There was just something about him, she'd said. His smile. No, that wasn't it. His manner. She'd liked his hands. How they were clean, soft. The way his shirts were ironed and crisp. He smelled of lemons, she'd said.

So, her place it was.

That was four months ago. It was not Riley's first affair. No sir-ee. But this one was young. Twenty-two. He knew there were risks involved. Twenty-two-year-old girls had nothing to lose. They were erratic. Impulsive. Crude. Demanding in attention and selfish in conversation. Yet he couldn't say no to her. She was so clear about what she wanted. And what she wanted was him. There was something about this girl who surfed for fun and fixed cars for a living, her long blonde hair and pale blue eyes, something that made logic — the kind of logic that kept Riley sharp and tough-minded in budgetary meetings with the American investors — seem superfluous.

The four months had sped by in a whirr, lunchtimes at her place, Sunday afternoons in a hotel down by the beach, a week-end away up the coast on the borrowed sailboat of a colleague, but now, this morning, he was right good and stuck. Why would Jack not dismiss him?

Riley thought of his personal assistant, Rose. Rose Finlayson. How Rose would already be at the office. She'd be talking on the phone to her friends or making herself tea or collecting the papers together that were lying across his desk from the evening before. Which papers would be there? Annual report. He and Chris Chatsworth had worked late on the annual report. Got it licked, almost. Chris Chatsworth could do numbers. Good, smart kid. Had a future at the company. His desk: its hard smoothness. The annual report. Had he separated out the notes from the working draft? If not, Rose might throw out their revision of the third-quarter numbers. Bugger.

He imagined Rose closing the lids on the cold Chinese takeaway and putting it all in the garbage, her lightly arthritic hands sweeping up the crumbs from the fortune cookies. His fortune had read, "All who know you, think you virtuous." *Whatever the hell that means,* Chris Chatsworth and he had laughed!

Suddenly, Jack stood and spoke. "I want you to leave her. Leave her and be with me. I can't go on with this shit."

Riley moved across the room and reached out his hand, touching Jack on the top of her head.

"Leave me alone!"

Her blonde hair. Some of it became stuck in her sudden gush of tears and matted against her face. What a mess. She was wearing one of his dress shirts. Her eyes were red when she looked up at him. It surprised him how she could shift from such pleasant smiles, making cups of tea, and idle chitchat about the beach or the car she was fixing yesterday, to such anger and outrage. How close love and hate were forced to live in this flat, he thought.

And he held onto this observation a moment longer than he might normally have done, to admire its evident insight. With his brain good and awake now, he revelled in the sheer power of being in possession of a muscular intellect. Being right was something he'd lived with all his life. Yes, he was ready for the day, for whatever it might throw his way.

"Go. Please leave. Get out."

There. That's what he'd been waiting for. He was dismissed.

"I'll come around after work. I'm sorry," he said.

Why did he say that? He regretted the words immediately. He'd opened his mouth and they'd just flown out. He couldn't come around after work. Vivian, his wife, likely knew what he was up to and he couldn't very well make up something else on such short notice. She allowed a certain amount of it, almost. But Riley had been doing a lot of lying recently on account of Jack. Too much of it, he suspected.

God, it *had* been four months now. No, he knew that Vivian wouldn't stand for it. Especially tonight. She'd asked him weeks ago to keep the tenth free. The Lovetrees were coming around for dinner. Oh, the bloody Lovetrees. He hated the Lovetrees. Vivian knew that. But Lillian Lovetree was one of Vivian's oldest friends. He owed it to Vivian to be home, fixing drinks, making small-bloody-talk with Brian Lovetree. He owed Vivian.

"Just go," said Jack. Then she spoke again, but it was to herself rather than him. "I wish *I* could go."

TO AN EXECUTIVE LIKE RILEY, always on the move, his car was his fortress. It was new and fast. It smelled as good to him each time he climbed inside as the day he'd driven it off the lot. Riley loved the way the world and all its petty problems just melted away when he drove. At least, they usually did. For a while he daydreamed, reminiscing about his old friend Kent Black from his Texas days; but he couldn't hold onto the reverie. Today, he couldn't shake what he'd talked himself into. He would have to get out of seeing Jack tonight. Should he phone her from the car, now? Perhaps Rose could do it for him? What's on first? Marketing with Chris Chatsworth, then a scheduled phone call with Dallas and Calgary, then drive all the way into the centre of Sydney for a meeting with a committee of stupid wankers from the state and three local governments. They were threatening court action if the refinery didn't develop a "more comprehensive" long-term environmental plan. Bloody greenie, Labor Party bludgers. They want to set "targets," for god's sake.

But Riley's mind soon returned to Jack. He couldn't shake the sound of Jack's voice. It *had* been less upset by the end. That was good. It had a touch of resignation to it. Perhaps she'd simply given up on him. That might be the best course of action. Perhaps it was time to move on. But then he thought of her in bed with him last night, her taut thighs, and grew less sure.

Riley drove out past the beach on his way to the office. The day stretched out to the horizon in a wide sweep that seemed to go on forever. He loved the sky down here, this far south of Sydney's core. Less smog. He was glad he'd moved. Life was different. The people were friendlier. He pulled the car over and got out. It was first thing in the morning but a Mr. Whippy truck had pulled up near the surf club and was selling drinks and chips to the kids on their way to school. He bought an orange juice and walked over to a bench. He had to clear his head of Jack before he went into the office.

The waves rolled in nice even lines, the white water bubbling, leaving trails of foam and streaks of itself marking up the deep blue of the sea. He knew now, he had not been thinking straight. He'd have to cancel on Jack, break his promise. He'd go home to the Lovetree dinner party. It might be the end of it with Jack.

Back in the car, along the stretch of road that ran out to the refinery, Riley slid in a tape. It was a compilation of *his* music. Great old country. The kind they didn't do anymore. Certainly not in Australia, at any rate. Well, he shouldn't say that. He didn't know that for sure. He'd never really looked into it. Not for years, at any rate. Perhaps things had changed? He would ask Rose if she knew of a good record store in Sydney that might have Australian country music. Perhaps he could get away to one of these stores after his meeting with the Labor bastards. Yes, that was an idea. Rose could call around a few places.

JACK STOOD IN FRONT of the mirror and let Riley's shirt fall to the ground. She was glad he was gone. She wanted to be by herself. A new song she liked was on the radio and she hummed along with it.

She ran her hands over her stomach, turned side on. Nothing yet. At least she hadn't felt sick this morning with him right there.

"THERE'S BEEN AN ACCIDENT," said Rose. Her face was not its usual sweet self. She was all smiles, normally. *Hi how are you I've cleaned your desk and would you like a coffee ... or maybe wait a bit.* That's what she'd usually say. She was an older woman whose confidence and good grooming always made Riley feel at his best. This morning, though, Rose was standing in front of the door to his office with a stony expression.

"What sort of accident?"

"Chris Chatsworth is inside. I just wanted to warn you."

Riley walked around Rose and into his office. Sitting, waiting for him, was Chris. As if he'd never moved on from their Chinese food and annual report draft last evening.

"One of the night-shift blokes died last night," said Chris as Riley sat down behind his desk.

"What?"

"His name was Frank Holts. He's only been with us for three weeks."

"What the hell happened?"

"Both unions are already here. The cops are down at the plant and some blokes from a special task force in Sydney are on their way. A Channel-bloody-Seven chopper has been circling all morning."

"What happened?"

"This Frank Holts bloke… he was checking valves on one of the empty tanks. See, they were siphoning last night." Chris Chatsworth's head fell into his hands.

"The through-pump was left engaged?" Riley felt suddenly sick. "My god, he drowned in the light sweet crude?"

Riley's head was spinning. He tried to imagine how this could have happened. With all the new safety procedures. But the more he learned from Chris Chatsworth, the more he understood all too well. It seemed perfectly logical. It had been a strange and emotional morning already at Jack's place, but now Riley was at work. *Get a grip, mate,* he told himself.

"Are we liable?" Riley asked.

"We're not in the wrong, Riley, technically," said Chris Chatsworth. "But we're ratshit one way or another. A bloke died while he was working. We're good and rooted."

"What do we know about him?"

"He's got a wife. I talked to her. The cops brought her here first thing this morning."

"What time did this happen?"

"And he has a three-year-old little girl."

"What time?"

"About eleven last night. You'd left about ten minutes before-hand. I was just finishing off the numbers in here. Heard the plant's emerg sirens go off. Jumped in the ute and raced down. The boys were great, Riley."

"They didn't prevent it!" Riley was shouting. "Did they! Well, Chris? Bloody unions make us do all this expensive safety shit, then they go kill a bloke. Dickheads."

"They had it emptied and him out of there in less than half an hour. We tried calling you … that's right … but your wife … She said she'd have you call us if you contacted her."

"Oh, shit."

"Listen, there are a pile of people who want to talk to you. Cops being the first ones."

"Shit."

"What are you going to say?" asked Chris.

"Nothing. Abso-bloody-lutely nothing. Neither will you. Don't talk to anyone."

Like most men of his age and stature, there were those crises that Riley liked to handle, and those he did not. The only real difference between the two varieties was location. If a crisis was at work, Riley was a major general. A discipli-narian. A logician. He almost relished this kind of triage. All around him, men would lose their heads, but not Riley. This was where he shone. The home front was another matter.

After Chris Chatsworth left the office and closed the door, Riley sat down behind his desk and took a long deep breath.

"Rose!"

"Yes?" She was at his door before he'd even finished hollering her name.

"Cancel everything in the book this morning. Call my wife and tell her I'm back from Melbourne. Tell her what's happened here. Be vague. Assure her I will be home for the dinner party with the Lovetrees."

"But you hate the Lovetrees."

"I know. I have to do it. Oh, right, but don't cancel the meeting in Sydney this afternoon. I have to go shit on those greenie pricks and now I'm really in the mood."

VIVIAN PLUCKED HER RECIPE folder from the shelf above the fridge.

In a small heavy saucepan with a tight-fitting lid, bring water to a boil with garlic, onion, cumin, coriander seeds, and salt. Stir in rice and cook, covered, over low heat 20 minutes. Stir in corn and cook, covered, 3 minutes, or until water is absorbed and rice is just tender. Fluff mixture with a fork and transfer to a large bowl to cool completely.

She stopped reading because the phone began to ring. "If that dickhead thinks he's getting out of this ..." Although Vivian was alone, she spoke this aloud. Out of habit she wiped her hands on her apron before picking up the phone.

"Vivian, it's Rose."

"Just a minute, I have to turn on the heat and … Right. I'm back."

"I'm afraid there's been some sort of accident down in the factory."

"Oh, dear. Is anyone hurt, Rose?"

"It's all a bit unclear at the moment. Riley is on his way down there now. He wanted me to ring you and let you know he's back from Melbourne. Oh, and that he's not forgotten about the dinner party you're having tonight."

Rose placed the phone back in its receiver. She looked briefly at her nails, at the red polish she'd applied this morning. Her computer had not yet been turned on. She'd spent the early part of her morning cleaning up Riley's desk, sighing to herself. Just as she'd expected, a complete mess had been left from them working late the night before.

She caught herself sighing again now. In Melbourne, indeed! How could Vivian put up with his endless infidelity? Then, as Rose had many times before, she came to the conclusion that Vivian must simply not know. Or not want to know. How could the woman be so gullible, so — as her own mother might have put it — light in the head?

AS RILEY STRODE ALONG through the plant, the men who worked the morning shift stood aside, silent as he passed. He didn't come down here much anymore. He recognised some of their faces from Christmas parties, from around the office when they had to report to personnel, a couple blokes, too, from The Workers Club.

Riley listened as a constable told him how things stood. Riley liked what he was hearing.

"Horrible accident, mate. Couldn't be helped. He was wearing a safety hat and had completed all the training only days before." The policeman spoke in grave tones.

Frank Holts's body was taken away. The news chopper stopped its circling only after Riley got a mate of his to ring another bloke who was high up at Channel Seven. "It's like Viet-fucking-nam down here, mate. Ring him and ask him to call off the chopper." Then, for good measure, he threw in: "It's upsetting the widow."

Riley called over the foreman and made arrangements for most of the men to take the day off. The foreman agreed they couldn't completely shut it down. That would take weeks of planning. But they could rotate off some of the blokes. Keep morale up, as much as possible.

"Also, Riley?" asked the foreman. "Some of the blokes want to know if they can help. Give money to the widow? Can they do that?"

"Might be distressing if they just start giving her twenties, mate," said Riley. "Listen, we should do something more orderly. Talk to Chris. Let's do a big chook raffle for her. The company will match whatever the blokes raise."

"Good idea. I'll speak to the boys."

They were approaching a group of the workers just now. They didn't look happy to see Riley. This would take more than a day off and a chook raffle to win them over.

"What was he like, this Frank Holts?" Riley asked the foreman, now within earshot of half a dozen of the morning shift.

"Quiet fella. Good bloke," said the foreman. Riley nodded.

"This cannot happen ever again, do you hear me? Comb the safety procedures. Talk to every bloke who works here. Get input from abso-bloody-lutely everyone. The cops will find out what went wrong. Your job is to make sure we fix the way we do things. Never again. Do you hear me?"

"Of course."

"Listen mate, Chris is coming down here for the afternoon. If anyone has any questions, put them to him. My door will be open all day tomorrow if anyone has any concerns. All day."

Riley left the foreman and the men. He walked over to the widow. She was a thin woman, dressed in a slight frock. She looked like she was sleepwalking.

"You have a little girl?" he said.

"Yes."

"What's her name?"

"Phillipa."

The woman hardly spoke. After a time, Riley simply said, "We'll do whatever we can to help you." He meant that. The stuff in front of the boys about making changes, fixing the problems. That was bullcrap. Riley knew that accidents just happen. Life's like that. But he would help the widow, as best he could.

"I EXPECT YOU BLOKES have heard what happened this morning at the refinery."

"Of course, Riley. We reckoned you might need to cancel."

"I saw the body. It was really awful," said Riley.

"Are you sure you want to do this?"

"I know you blokes have been trying to get me into this room for months. Here I am. Let's go through it."

The meeting with the labour mob went very well. In the car on the way over, Riley had decided to turn his bad morning into a good afternoon. He played the dead-worker card with sorrow and humanity. Riley knew some of the blokes who were in the room. He knew if they themselves had not, then their brothers and fathers and mates were working similar jobs. He knew they'd taken the accident to heart, and he also knew that a sympathetic approach, getting it right out in the open, showing them — a hidden until now — side of him that was humane and vulnerable, would help matters a great deal.

His long-term strategy was to stall these fellas. They wanted to regulate the living shit out of the refinery. Monitor every litre of crap that he was pumping into the ocean. Stuff that. He wouldn't let them near it. If he was to actually do what they were asking, he'd have to pay to store or dispose of the waste. The cost of that would finish the company in Australasia. Then where would all their "brothers" on his factory floor be? No. That wasn't going to happen. He had decided in the car on the way over to listen to everything they had to say. To act as if what they said was news to him. Interesting news. To try and find something small he could do right away to show goodwill. Then to promise to study the larger issues … for as long as bloody possible … preferably until the world came up with a viable alternative to fossil-fucking-fuel.

And this was exactly how the meeting went. There was only one bloke in the room, Red Martin, who saw right through Riley's bullshit. Tough, smart character. But that's where the morning's accident helped him. Red would have normally called Riley on his stalling tactics. Today, given the tragedy, Riley pretended he was simply not in the best frame of mind to be making the big decisions they were asking of him. So even old Red was forced to give Riley the benefit of the doubt.

What a bunch of mugs. It'll be another bloody year before they get me in that room again, thought Riley on his way out into the Sydney sunshine. He thought about popping up to the top floor of the ANA hotel for a Crown Lager. Loosen his tie for the first time since he'd tightened it, at Jack's, this morning. Instead, he dug around in his pocket for a slip of paper. There, scrawled in Rose's last-minute handwriting, was the name and address of a record store that sold country music. That was the kind of sweet woman Rose was. Even on a day like today, nothing was too much trouble.

Riley drove through the city to Newtown, parked, and entered the shop. He found a gold mine. He spent an hour flipping through the records. Great old country music. Lots of it.

"Anything Australian?" he'd asked. And they had that too. He bought several hundred dollars' worth of music. Old standards, and new local outfits.

As a young man, Riley had spent two years in Texas working on a rig. There was still, if you listened carefully, an occasional twang to the odd word Riley used. They'd been great years for him. He'd met blokes from all over the States working on that rig. His two closest friends were Kent Black, the loud-mouthed Alaskan, and "Bull" J.S. Friday from Birmingham. Together, the three of them had done it all.

That was how he'd got his start in the oil business. He'd been traveling in the States. Not really knowing what he wanted to do with his life, he took a job on a rig. There he learned about life, drinking. How to influence other men. In Texas they were tough. Tougher than even here in Australia; more stupid, though. He'd avoided tight situations many a time out of sheer smarts the other blokes lacked. Riley chalked up his grit and tough talk to what he learned in those two years.

Most of all, he remembered his Texas days fondly for the music he grew to love. Listening to country music, he'd worked, drank, lost his virginity to a half-Mexican beauty up against the back wall in a rancher's barn. She'd ridden the young Riley like she wanted to hear the crowd roar and take home the money. Least, that's how he remembered it these days.

RILEY WAS HUMMING a country song when he opened the door. He could hear threads of Vivian's laughter. She was out on the verandah with the Lovetrees.

"Here he is!" they all said when he entered.

"G'day, Brian," and Riley shook Brian Lovetree's limp hand, doing his best to crush it and make Brian feel like the poofter he was. "Lillian, darling," and he pulled Lillian Lovetree towards him and gave her a big kiss on the mouth like he always did. The kind of kiss intended to remind her instantly of the pool change room at her old house, the smell of chlorine, the weight of him on top of her as they went at it on the pile of boogie boards and life jackets. "How are ya, doll?"

"We're only in town for one night," said Brian. "We're on our way up to the Sunshine Coast."

Riley excused himself and went inside to pour a drink. Vivian joined him, taking his arm, whispering to him, "You alright? Rose rang. It was on the news."

"Who'd drive from Melbourne to the Sunshine-fuckin-Coast?" Riley was speaking through his clenched teeth. "Cheapskates."

"*I* invited them to stay over," she said in her friend's defence.

"They *are* cheap. Brian Lovetree is the largest soft-cocked, pain in the ass you could ever hope to meet." He'd said *pain in the ass* because he'd been thinking of Texas, of himself as a younger, carefree man on the drive home. He suspected Vivian would pick up on his American phrase, and its implications of where his mind had recently been, immediately.

Riley had always hated Brian Lovetree. High school teacher. Worked about two hours a day and complained about how hard it was the other six. Glorified babysitter. Got about three months off a year. Taught geography or social science, whatever the hell that was. Got his information out of high school textbooks, but acted like he was personal advisor to the minister of foreign bloody affairs. Up-himself know-it-all.

"I've made a lot of food. I hope everyone is hungry!" said Vivian, leaving Riley's side, waltzing out to the verandah. The doorbell rung. "I'll get it," she said, without losing her stride, posture or tone.

Vivian re-entered the room again just as Riley had finished mixing his drink. He looked up at her.

"There's someone at the door to see you, Riley," she said,

"Please hurry. We're all hungry." She smiled at him with bared teeth.

Riley walked over to the front door and opened it to find Jack standing there.

"You were supposed to come over tonight," she began.

"Why did you come?" His voice, a loud whisper. "You can't be here."

"I have to talk to you," she said.

"But not now."

"You have to help me."

"What?"

"I want to leave. I have to go away somewhere," Jack pleaded.

"What?"

"If you don't help me get out of this place, I'm going to tell everyone about us."

Riley stepped across the threshold and shut the door behind his back. He reached for Jack's shoulder.

"Jack! What are you talking about?"

"Can you help me go away, far away?"

"Well, probably, but Jack, why? Why do you want to go?"

"Just help me, okay?"

So Riley promised he'd come around to her place tomorrow. He promised he'd help her leave. He had no idea what was wrong or why she wanted to go, but on the face of it, it didn't seem like such a bad idea if she was going to start coming around to his house while the Lovetrees were on the verandah impatient to begin their dinner.

AS THE EVENING ROLLED ON, Riley began to yawn and check his watch. Before long he excused himself and, taking the stairs two at a time, went up to bed, leaving Brian with the two women.

"Brian honey," said Lillian. "Why don't you pop off to bed too? Give the girls a chance to gossip a bit, alone. Go on. I'll be up soon." And so Brian padded up the stairs.

"Riley looks tired," said Lillian, adopting a more confidential tone. Then she paused. "You were in the kitchen, but Riley did it again. Went to great lengths to tell Brian about how late and how hard he worked at the office last night. Why must he always ride Brian about being a teacher? Could you speak to him, Viv? Teaching isn't easy. Brian does work hard, you know."

"Of course he works hard," said Vivian. "Riley can't help being a bastard. It's part of his charm." She laughed a little. But, inwardly, Vivian was not assessing Riley's poor behaviour towards Brian. Nor was she revisiting her long-held suspicion that her husband and best friend have a secret all of their own. No, her mind had clamped onto Riley's working late at the office. He'd not been to Melbourne. That had been another of Rose's lies. He'd never be able to get away with as much as he did if that sour old bitch wouldn't be so obliging, so eager to cover his tracks. What had she ever done to Rose to provoke such effortless betrayal? All it took for the woman to lie, it seemed, was the promise of a paycheque. How, Vivian wondered, could Rose live with herself?

JACK TURNED OFF HER TELEVISION. The man who had drowned in oil at the refinery this morning was all over the news. She hadn't heard until now. She listened to the man's wife talk as she held her little girl, tightly.

Jack had rung in sick to work and had spent the day thinking. She had spread all her photographs across her bed. They made her cry and cry. Old friends from school who had long ago moved away. Her sister, her parents, her old dog. Boyfriends who had come and gone. Who was she? She didn't know anymore.

A baby was growing inside her. A life. She would have to give it a name. What, what would she call it? How can someone who doesn't know who she is name someone else? There was no one she wanted to tell of her baby. No one she felt she could tell. Not her parents, or younger sister, or friends. Certainly not Riley. She decided then and there to never tell any of them. She made a promise to herself to go it alone. It was a promise she would keep. But now she just wanted to run. Outrun this feeling she couldn't shake. It was a feeling unlike any she'd ever known, and it would be years before she was able to gave it a name, call it for what it was. Shame.

Tonight, however, it was dark outside. Her street was quiet but for the hum of the electric lights. She looked to the stars and the moon. Jack felt like the whole world was out there, but it was no longer waiting for her.

THE NEXT MORNING, on his way to Jack's, Riley stopped by the beach. He bought an orange juice from the Mr. Whippy truck and sat on the wall beside the surf club. The swell was huge today. The beach was crammed with surfers all jostling for waves, flinging their boards in the air. Jack should be out there, he thought. Not waiting at home for him to come over and fix all her problems. She should be out having fun. That's what he'd done at her age, gone to Texas and had fun. Why didn't she just face her problems? He'd known twenty-two-year-olds were trouble. Well, maybe *he* was *her* problem. Maybe she sensed they were over. She was upset at losing him, likely. He could understand that.

At that moment Riley's old buddy from his Texas days, Kent Black, popped into his head. He smiled. He'd not talked to Kent in more than a year, but it never mattered. Kent was the kind of mate who would lend a hand and not ask questions. He owned his own mining operation up in Alaska now. Ran half the state. He'd give Kent a ring. See if he couldn't fix Jack up with a job there, in Alaska. They could cook something up together to sort her out and get her on her way.

The morning sun was working its way up in the sky and the juice was going down smoothly. Life, thought Riley, is a bit of a puzzle. But there's always a solution. Always. Why didn't everyone see this? He laughed to himself a little. Because most people are, essentially, stupid. You just have to meet it all head on and figure things out as you go, remember who is number one, stay healthy, and keep focused. Remain a step ahead of everyone else. It's not hard at all. No, thought Riley, life is easy and good. Easy and good.

ALASKA

AMANDA REMEMBERS THE DAY now as she always has. It begins in her bedroom, trying on tops, deciding which one might be the best. Then rummaging through the family's hall closet to find the least daggy beach towel. The beginnings of this day could still play in Amanda's mind as if it had only just taken place, as if the twenty years of her life that followed meant nothing at all.

As Amanda lowers herself to a sit, the old boards on her verandah give a little. She adjusts the bucket of water and ice-cubes, sinks her feet into it. The gum trees in her garden send a swelling of sorrow through her whole body. This has happened a lot lately. Unaccountable bursts of emotion. Today, the trees, of all things. She feels a kindred spirit with them, the way they twist up under themselves in the heat, the bark curling off in long tubes like waves breaking down the beach.

As it did back then, the hard sun smacks the world about her with an arrogant hand, beating at her neck. Gradually, Amanda grows cross at the weather, becomes beside herself at the stiff light, can't think for the deadening heat. For a long displeasing minute, Amanda believes all cruelty in Australia comes from the sun itself. Amidst a hopeless life you'll blame anyone, anything. The sun, fate, at times even Jack herself.

The heat is in collusion with the haze of the morning and fume of Sydney off in the distance. Amanda drops her head and she rubs her eyes until, eventually, her anger subsides.

She regains her sharpness, admitting to herself, quietly, there is simply no one to blame.

When Amanda brings her sister Jack to mind now, she usually remembers how Jack would look up through her long, blonde hair while she waxed her surfboard in tight circles. Jack had spoken and moved in ways Amanda's small world wasn't ready for then. It was as if Jack had had an inside tip on the outcome and had resigned herself to it. She was going to run amok until her very last minute.

Jack had lived in her own flat, fixed cars for a living, had sex and surfed, drank. She could be relied upon for anything. She never took no for an answer. About anything, from anybody. She wasn't stubborn, she was persuasive, and had an attitude that was much better in your corner than someone else's.

"My mate can't make it. Want to come instead?" Jack had said to Amanda over the phone, in her way — which was with a mischievous lilt to her voice, saying nothing important, implying endless possibilities.

Amanda's heart had skipped that day, thumping inside her chest at the thought of driving out of Sydney, south along the coast until Jack spotted the waves she wanted. Jack was the only girl Amanda knew who surfed. As Amanda had put on a bit of lippy, she'd forecast the day in her mind. They'd find a pub to eat at, sit outside, drink a beer, or a lemon, lime and bitters if Jack wouldn't let her have a beer. Sometimes they'd drink beer together, other times Jack would say, "Rack off, Amanda. You're not old enough."

There was always a chance with Jack. The possibility of fun lurked within every moment. But, Amanda — only fourteen at the time — sensed that things were changing between them. Amanda had begun to feel Jack was keeping secrets from her. Jack was twenty-two then, much older than she was, and didn't come round as much.

The heat, Amanda thinks now as she looks at the ice cubes floating about her legs, the heat makes me maniacal. My life would be inexplicable to an Eskimo. She concedes that the arctic is equally unimaginable to her. One day I'll travel to Alaska. She tells herself this on days like today. Days when the heat makes it so hard to breathe. And it was this, the blazing heat, that she hadn't counted on as they'd piled into Jack's Toyota on that day so long ago, and set off.

"I hope my surfboard's strapped to the roofrack tight enough," laughed Jack as she threw the car in gear and squealed the tires.

As Jack and Amanda worked their way out of Sydney, the morning sun grew oppressive. Amanda had pinched two apples and a Kit Kat from the fridge, but by the southern suburb of Engadine the chocolate was softening and the apples were beginning to roast in the back seat. Amanda dug around as Jack tried to change gears and steer.

"Sit down, you mole," joked Jack.

"But they'll be ruined. Do you want the Kit Kat or an apple?"

"I'm not hungry."

Amanda had really wanted the Kit Kat. She'd have one of the apples now instead, saving the Kit Kat, in case Jack wanted it later.

On the radio, The Police sang, "Walking on the Moon," and Amanda worked her way through the apple. Being together like this reminded Amanda of when they were kids. Now, Jack went everywhere with her mates, almost never including her. Amanda looked at Jack smoking a Winfield, her golden arm resting on the car window, a single white stripe of zinc cream across her nose. Brand new Ray Bans, imported from America.

"I want a Corvette," Jack had said.

Jack's hair was white blonde. Her lips tensed around the cigarette, and wrinkles played across her brow as she negotiated the traffic. It was the same face she wore when she was playing pinball. Jack would jab at the machine, all hips and pelvis. She drank hard. She never gossiped. Her boobs were great. She always remembered Amanda's birthday. Jack was intense, magnetic. Jack was perfect. To be asked to come along surfing, this was a giant step. Things were getting back to normal. But what *was* normal?

Jack had moved out of their family home not long after her eighteenth birthday — years ago now. It hadn't been an upsetting event for Amanda. Even she — a girl at the time — had been able to see Jack's pride at being grown up, to have her own place, a fitting status to accompany her new job as an apprentice mechanic. But there had been talk of Amanda coming over for visits, to muck about with her older sister. The change had been presented to her as only a technicality. These visits almost never happened.

Amanda stands, stepping out of the bucket of water, and slips on her sandals. As if this day were prone to miracles, her feet dry by the time she does up the second buckle. It's so hot. I must get the mail, she thinks. I must make myself something to eat.

The family had received the odd postcard from Jack over the years. They followed her racing career during those first few seasons she was on the amateur circuit in the States. Omaha, Flagstaff, Boulder. Jack was a presence in their lives, always there, talked about at Christmastime or when they were reminded of something she used to do or say.

Amanda's the only one left now to keep these thoughts alive. Both her parents are dead. Four years this January since her father passed. Amanda's still in the family home. Keeps the family bakery going. Never married, but — as she likes to joke with her favourite customers as she hands them warm sandwich loaves and sticky finger buns, or fresh vanilla slices and jam rolls — never divorced either.

Walking down the path, Amanda adjusts her hat forward. Its wide brim casts shade across her face and shoulders. At the mailbox, at its steely lip and dark slot, Amanda looks up and out along the esplanade. Heat waves shimmer as if Australia is having a migraine. She looks away, down at the ground, at spat-out gobs of chewing gum which have liquefied into black moles, pockmarking the cement, at a discarded cake of surfboard wax that has melted and fills the air with its coconut perfume. Tahiti. Tar-heat-y. The cement glimmers and bows. Her skin is burning through her dress as if she is exposed. What I would do for some cool shade, some relief. Oh, the heat. Lay me in an igloo, lay me down on an iceberg and let me freeze to death. Yes, one day. One day I will go to Alaska and let snow melt in my mouth, pack ice around my body. There would be worse ways to go than being enclosed in ice, slowly dreaming yourself away.

The letter about Jack has arrived, just as the telephone message had said it would.

Nothing moves down the esplanade and Amanda gulps, trying to take in air. Her dress is untied at the back. Her shallow breaths labour profoundly. The letter is in her hand. She should walk back to the house, back to the bucket of water — now in need of more ice cubes — and put her feet in it and read the letter.

Jack was based out of Anchorage. That's what they were led to believe, and what they told people when asked. She raced stock cars and dirt bikes for a few years but always went back to Alaska. She worked for an oil company for a time. Then she married Brett. Several years later she telephoned to tell them of her divorce. She wrote some years after that and mentioned towards the end that she was married again. They never learned the name of the last man. That was about the time when Jack stopped her occasional phone calls and birthday cards.

Amanda can see Jack's legs working the pedals of the car like it was yesterday. Jack was steering, changing gears. They were on a bush road, going to no beach in particular, just south.

"I'll take that apple now," Jack had said.

Jack had blue eyes. Her skin tanned perfectly even all over, a golden copper colour. When she smiled boys were helpless.

For some time they had driven in silence. And Amanda watched Jack's legs give and take as she engaged the clutch, as Jack bit into her apple, as she sighed and rolled up her window when dust and the smell of shit clouded over and enveloped their car from the truck full of pigs they were following. But they finally passed it when the road straightened out. Jack immediately wound down the window all the way again and hung her elbow out, the rushing wind blowing her hair, filling the car with good smells once more — Jack's apple, the sea, the bush.

It was summer, and Amanda was in love with her big sister Jack, horribly, deeply in love. It wasn't fair that she didn't come round much anymore. Jack used to play with her, take her to the shops on the handlebars of her push bike. Jack would always say to her friends, "Amanda is coming too. She's cool. She won't say nothing."

When they were even younger, Jack would take her to the Royal Easter Show and let her get too many sample bags. They would come home and make piles of all the lollies. They would count them out. See who got more. Then Jack would begin an elaborate game of trading.

"My Freddo Frog is worth your seven Red Skins."

They would swap back and forth in a drawn-out game that Jack would change the rules of, as they went along. By the end Amanda would have most of the lollies, Jack having traded all the ones Amanda liked and accepted from her all the ones she didn't. Hanging out with Jack. Laughing. The day could not have been better.

Amanda looks up from her verandah and sees a woman walking towards her on the esplanade. She is tall and has a long gait but moves slowly under the sun's weight. She is the right age. Amanda watches her approach. The woman's thin body reminds Amanda of pistons, of a greased machine whose job it is to work hard. The woman is taut and purposeful, graceful and calm. She looks beautiful. Amanda turns over the letter in her hands. Its stamp depicts the stars and stripes fluttering in the breeze. The postmark is Fairbanks, Alaska.

Today, in heat similar to that long-ago day, Amanda can taste the browning apple in her mouth, hear Sting's syrupy voice on the tinny AM radio, feel the sticky seats of the Toyota. She recalls the afternoon Jack first arrived home with the car.

"It's finished! I did it." She was like a showroom model, standing beside this glinting car. But it wasn't new at all. It had suffered a bad accident. Jack had bought it for a bargain from the owner who had thought it a write-off. Jack fixed it up herself. All the bodywork. Found the missing parts. Did the panel beating. To her, it was a work of art.

The tall woman passes Amanda on the esplanade and Amanda clutches at the letter, pulling it into her. The woman nods politely, throwing Amanda a half-smile as if to say, "Mate, it's hot!" Amanda returns the stranger's smile and continues to watch her from behind. The woman's calf muscles are long and defined. Amanda always looks, prepared to make adjustments for age and fashion. But it's never Jack.

The letter talks of the avalanche in general terms. The temperature of the day, the conditions. All figures are in Fahrenheit and mean nothing to her. The landscape is not carefully described. Amanda does not in truth know what a forest of fir trees looks like. And who are these three men with Jack? Is one her second husband? When did she become an experienced mountaineer and guide?

That summer day, Jack had pulled the Toyota over in a little town, the name of which Amanda had never heard before. They sat in a park across the road from the beach.

"Waves look good," Jack said, her eyes scanning the horizon for incoming sets.

"I'll get us Paddle Pops?" Amanda had offered.

Amanda walked across the grass, leaving Jack sitting on the edge of the town's large, stone war memorial. Amanda bought them ice blocks, a bag of Chicken Cheezles and a Fanta.

She was just buying stuff. Happy purchasing things with her pocket money for them to share.

"I'm going to go out for a surf," Jack said when Amanda returned, taking the ice block from her, eating quickly. She was always eager to get into the water.

"I might have a swim later," Amanda said as Jack began to prepare to go surfing. "Where are the flags?"

"Dunno. Waves are working perfectly. There's a few blokes catching lefts there off that sandbank." Jack had only the surf on her mind.

The day beat down on them. From the war memorial, Amanda squinted at the oppressive light dancing off the waves, reflecting whiteness on car windscreens and hubcaps and mirrors. A mother and daughter were taking an outdoor shower together in the small park that led down to the beach. The little girl was standing stock-still, the water falling over her body as her mother rinsed inside her own swimsuit and ran her fingers through her hair. Seagulls scabbed about for fallen chips. Boys with surfboards walked in pairs in and out of the water, looking serious, as if they would always live in this moment.

Soon, Jack was unleashing her board from the roof of the Toyota, unsheathing it from its bag, giving it a quick wax, and walking down to the water's edge. Amanda looked on.

She had never stopped looking on. Even now, four weeks after Jack's accident, after Jack lay buried alive under a mountainside of snow and rock, she looks on. Waiting for her sister to come back, to come home. Amanda scoops out a piece of floating ice from the bucket of water and rubs it up along the skin of her leg. She looks on as if their day together, so long ago, were still occurring. The little girl showering. The mother rinsing herself off. Jack by the water's edge doing up her leg rope. The long list of dead names commemorated on the war memorial.

She, Amanda, is the last witness to Jack's life. Her real life. Not her Alaskan life. That was just a dream. Amanda feels she is trapped back there watching Jack surfing, still licking at her frozen vanilla Paddle Pop, its whiteness forever cold in her mouth. Why didn't she stop her, somehow make her stay?

While Jack surfed, Amanda had wandered down the street. The striped awnings were fully extended on the shop fronts, protecting them from the sun. On the corner, next to a big old two-storey pub with Victorian wrought-iron fencing in the upper verandah, she saw an interesting shop. A sort of gallery. A big, one-roomed place, with local artists' work on the walls: acrylic gullies with ghost gums, grubby bush with distant windmills, or cattle, or wallabies, yellow rock, picturesque creeks and trees so balanced and proportioned that if they were words, rather than images, they'd be palindromes.

When had they stopped playing the palindrome game together?

"A Toyota. Hey, that's one!" Jack had cried out one day. The funniest palindrome ever was, "Kayak salad Alaska yak." That one was Jack's. At the time Amanda had believed Jack, when Jack said she'd made it up. Amanda had been astonished as she worked her way through the letters backwards and forwards, amazed at Jack, that it actually worked. She later realized, of course, that Jack must have found it in a book somewhere. But as girls, being silly on a car trip curled up in the backseats, or on Christmas Eve unable to sleep, it was a game they'd play together. They'd collected so many at one time, slipping backward and forward letter by letter.

Lately, Amanda feels her mind too is slipping, changing. It is becoming more difficult to hang on to all the details. The exactness of her memory is melting away at the edges.

Amanda had regarded the art in the gallery. It reminded her of their mother's tea-towels. The shop also sold greeting cards, and carvings made out of indigenous wood and pieces of quartz mounted on stands and silver jewellery handmade by "Natasha." The name was written in gold lettering on little mauve cards dangling from the quartz.

Amanda realized she was shopping for Jack. She was gazing at the knick-knacks, looking to buy Jack something. Just a small present. She fingered the quartz. Not really Jack's cup of tea. In fact, nothing in the little shop seemed quite right. So Amanda decided against it all in the end. There would be another beach. Other towns.

"I thought you were never coming back," said Jack, glancing up at the list of names of fallen soldiers from the Boer War. Jack was still wet. "Don't go off like that. Just wait 'til I finish next time. I want hot chips."

Sometimes Amanda catches herself smiling along, mimicking herself, swept up in her memories of Jack. She blesses the verandah as she catches the first tiny gust of a cooler breeze. She cups water up over her arms, spreading the coolness on herself like ointment. She is in the same dress today — the long loose one with big flowers on it — that Jack had bought for her later that very day. It had gone way out of style, but has lately come right back in. She has always kept it regardless, and wears it every so often. Today it seemed like the right thing to put on.

The letter goes on to say that on behalf of the park's superintendent and staff, they are deeply sorry for her loss. That Jack was a fine employee and that she would be missed by all who knew her and called her friend. Enclosed is a local news clipping that covers the rescue efforts in the days following the avalanche. There is a small photograph, a headshot of Jack, lifted from her driver's licence. It has reproduced badly, but at least it is *something*. Jack looks older. Her hair is still long. She isn't smiling, though. Amanda looks deep into her sister's face.

They had wandered about the town, looking for a milk bar to buy hot chips, but had ended up instead slipping into a clothing store.

"Are you finished buttoning up in there?" Jack said over the change room door. Amanda emerged into the light wearing the dress. "Oh, now that one," Jack had said with a half-smile, "that one I like. Got paid yesterday. I'll buy it for you."

It gives her goosebumps to remember Jack saying that, the words covering Amanda's body in icy prickles, as her arms drip-dry quickly in the heat. She needs more ice in the bucket. It has almost all melted. She stands and goes inside to the freezer, a billow of coldness hitting out against her face. Amanda puts the letter and newspaper clipping down on her kitchen table.

On her return to the verandah, the strange woman is no longer in her line of sight. Her absence, the empty esplanade, shakes Amanda out of her daze. The letter is back in her hand. Somehow she's picked it up again. She brings it to her face, touching it against her cheek momentarily, trying to pull something of Jack closer to her. How long did she survive taking in shallow, ever colder breaths? Days, a week, long enough to endure loneliness, to look back and regret?

She dumps the ice in the bucket and steps in. Amanda feels light-headed, weak, and she swoons a little. She needs something to eat. Yes, she's not eaten today. First she will go and make herself some tea and toast. A poached egg perhaps. Can I actually stand to boil water in this heat? Perhaps just a piece of fruit, an orange or an apple.

Somewhere along the list of instructions to herself she faints. Falls forward to her knees, then onto her front, in a timeless room she falls like ice as it hits the water in a million splashes without witness, melting about her face as she wriggles. Jack, the ice is melting. She calls this, feels the cold, the temperature now indistinguishable from the surrounding air. The dark yellow light, but the shade is nice. I am taking off. Don't laugh at me. Jack, this is chilly. Do you know heat anymore? Why don't you come?

It is only a moment; it is the sleep of a lifetime. It forces her to the centre of everything. She wakes remembering absolutely nothing.

Having decided to wear her new dress right away, they almost skipped out along the street. They found Jack a milk bar. Back in front of the war memorial, Jack was eating her hot chips and was telling Amanda of a kiss she'd had recently. Jack spoke of her own mouth as if it were someone else's. Her description was mesmerizing. It was the first time they'd talked like this, about boys, about love.

Jack had thought the kiss perfect in the after moments. It was one of those few kisses so exactly right, Jack said, that she could remember every slick, salty moment of it. Listening to Jack, eating warm chips together, Amanda become lost in Jack's telling. The sharing of it made the kiss linger about them, as if the thing had lasted forever. Indeed, the longer they spoke of it, the more it swelled about them in the air.

As they walked back to the car, Jack was still on about the kiss, Amanda's feet hardly touched the ground and she felt the gorgeous weight of desire press outward from deep inside her. God, the feel and taste of it is still ready at her lip all these years later. They'd climbed back into the Toyota and headed farther south.

Jack was beautiful. She'd laughed into the summer air, her window down as they continued their trip south, away from Sydney, the music blaring, both singing along. She was an apprentice mechanic at the local Toyota dealer. Even in overalls with grease on her cheek and neck, she was the girl every boy wanted. She was the grand prize. The name you wanted to scrawl in paint on the back of The Workers Club, carve along with your own initials into a Moreton Bay fig. She was tops. She was firm. A sort. A looker. She, the beloved older sister. She, who was about to leave forever. If only Amanda had known that at the time. But what could she have done to stop Jack?

They had rounded a bend and the road dipped away, winding down a headland. The radio signal started to break up and Jack flicked it off with a sigh. To their right, the sea. Its endlessness and prominence made it invisible to Amanda. It was something so abundant, so present, to be without it would never have occurred to her. Even driving with Jack to find the best waves, she didn't appreciate it.

Amanda did not want this day of independence, this day of
them to slow down or change direction or slip into the mundane.
She did not want Jack's attention to turn to the matters that
usually filled her life — fixing cars, all Jack's mates, and the endless parade of boys and their advances. The signal was lost on
the radio but Amanda wanted to keep driving until they ran
out of road heading south, she wanted to keep singing, filling
up her lungs with air.

"What kind of songs?" asked Jack, lighting a Winfield.

"Any songs. What do you know?"

"I can't sing. Have you ever heard me sing?"

"You just were."

"With the radio? That's different."

Amanda sensed a defensive thread to Jack's comment and
her face fell. Jack must have seen this because she back-pedalled.

"How about this, then." Jack looked off down the road into
the distance, searching for the words in her memory, and when
they came, they came long and cool and complete. She sang
almost all of an AC/DC song. Amanda wasn't sure which one,
but the words were familiar. Jack did the drum parts on the
dash with her index fingers. Used a different voice, a higher one,
for the chorus and waved her arms about in parts to help herself along with the guitar solo. She got stuck eventually and they
laughed as if they were in their own world, as if they were just
girls again, in the back seat of their parents' car, or hiding under
the trundle bed, or eating lollies pinched from their mother's
purse that were supposed to be for later — the taste of them
sweet and naughty.

The bush was hilly now, rolling almost. Bits of sand hill and stubby trees scoured the distance as they wound down the coast between headlands of rock and cliff, down to the heaving sea below. To their right was a creek, and there were benches and built-in barbecues and when Amanda pointed this out, Jack swerved, braked and pulled over to the side of the road.

"Come on!" Jack said and hoisted herself over the fence. Down at the creek, time and weather just fell away. They sat in shade and watched as a tree full of rosellas burst into the sky, sweeping around, returning to where they came. A rock wallaby hopped out for a minute before seeing them on the other side of the stream and taking off, frightened.

"Amanda, I got a new job."

"Really?"

"With an oil company."

"Doing what?"

"Apprentice mechanic, the same."

Jack took out a Winfield and lit it. As she smoked, her eyes scanned the bush for the wallaby. "This job. It's in Alaska. In America. I haven't told anyone yet. Just you."

Alaska. She'd only ever said the word aloud before giggling. *Kayak salad Alaska yak.* The idea of Jack going far away filled Amanda with a pang of panic and delight all at once. Mainly, because she was the first to know. She wanted to tell someone. She felt like she was ten years old with a great secret that only her best friend in the whole world could possibly understand the meaning of, or be trusted with. She felt the desire to tell it swell up inside her. But the person who she wanted to confide in, she quickly realized, was Jack herself. What she had just learned began to sink down into her stomach. Amanda burst into tears.

Jack smiled, a little apologetically. The kind of smile she might have worn if she'd just pulled out a sliver from Amanda's hand, or was brushing Amanda's hair and had worked out the last big knot. "There. That wasn't so bad, was it?" was what the smile said. Jack leapt to her feet.

"C'mon. I'm bored." She began to stride back to the car. Amanda followed, trying to keep up.

"An angry southerly buster is working its way up the coast from Victoria," was one of the last things they'd heard before they'd lost the radio signal. This wasn't surprising to either of them. The day had turned out to be well into the thirties. A stinker.

After the creek, they had climbed back into the Toyota and driven further south. They'd found a hidden beach that Jack had heard rumours about. A deserted right hand break kept her busy for much of the afternoon while Amanda collected shells on the beach, tanned, went for a swim, before finally sitting in the car. Amanda searched the dial and found a new station on the radio, which she listened to as she ate the soft Kit Kat and read a copy of *Dolly* she discovered under the seat. Jack reads *Dolly*? Must have been someone else's.

Soon Jack's mates would know about Alaska. There would be goodbye parties and then ... and then she would leave. Amanda considered the silence after Jack was gone. It would be long and deep and it would be a hole she could never fill. She didn't want to begin it, Jack's leaving. Maybe they wouldn't go back. They could sleep on the beach together. Build a fire. Jack even had a lighter. Amanda went to ask Jack about it.

The first wisps of stormy relief were in the air as she reached out her hand for Jack, gently. Jack had come out of the water and lain down on the deserted beach. She was sunbathing, almost asleep, stretched out on the towel soaking up the heat as she dried off. Her board shorts were still wet from the sea and they were tight around her legs. The deserted beach gave away to nothing. No one but them mattered at that moment. She reached for Jack.

Jack leapt up as if she'd been stung. She tried to speak, angry. She raised her arm at Amanda, about to swat her, but stopped short, bursting into tears which ended as quickly as they started.

"Just fucking leave me alone, alright? I wanted to have one last surfing trip and now you've …" Jack stopped. She looked to the sky, then down. She laughed at Amanda, not maliciously, but not without some pity either. "You need me gone. You do. Trust me."

Amanda fell down onto the sand. She watched as Jack grabbed her board and tore up the beach. Jack flung open the door to the Toyota, rolled her surfboard into the cloth cover, and fastened it onto the roof rack. She climbed into the car, started it, wound down the window.

"C'mon!" she screamed out at Amanda.

Amanda just sat there in the sand.

"It's gunna teem." Jack wasn't really cross; Amanda could tell that much. "Look!" Jack pointed at the sky. "A southerly is coming." Amanda just kept sitting. "Fine."

Jack drove off down the empty road.

Amanda had wanted to move but it felt like she had sand in her undies. They were all twisted around, itchy. So she stood and walked down into the sea, lifting her dress off at the shore. Squatting among the small waves, Amanda fixed herself a bit, let the water rinse her, brushing out the sand.

It only rained for a moment, but the water came in hard fat drops. Then it stopped abruptly, and the stilled storm produced a sinking, slanted yellow light. A black cloud swooped in from the northeast. Amanda waded out of the sea, picking up her dress on the beach, pulling it over her head. She was caught.

Hailstones the size of fists knocked her down, leaving marks on her skin the shape of bright red apples; the air chilled and bit at her, and in less than a moment, it was a full onslaught, mortar fire, a stoning, the nearest tree a shapeless, hopeless distance away.

Amanda tried to cover her head with her hands. She fell down onto the beach, sobbing, "Stop it, stop," into the sand, the ice belting against her neck, cracking against her back and forearms in relentless waves that she thought would never end like the moments leading up to a collision of two cars, or a deafening sound signalling something unidentifiable that you can't escape. The stones fell and fell and bounced off her, and she cried at the stinging and at Jack for driving away, for going to Alaska, and at her whole pathetic, misfortunate life as the cannonballs of ice beat her.

Then Jack was there again, holding her surfboard above the two of them.

"You're crazy!" she was saying, holding Amanda with one arm, the other keeping the surfboard balanced above their heads as a shield. "What are you thinking?"

It ended in a quieting of stones. They lessened for a moment, then stopped altogether. Jack dropped the board.

For as far as Amanda could see Australia was white. Even the sea was a slush of floating ice. Yes, the sea was suddenly something foreign; the thickened waves drew up to the carpet of whiteness, crystal and frozen, and took the whiteness on the edge back into itself. The beach wore a blanket of ice. The sun came out from behind the last of the black cloud and changed the light.

"What were you thinking?" Jack asked again. The two of them remained there for several minutes, not saying a word.

"Look Jack," Amanda said in a whisper after a time, "the ice is melting."

Now, Amanda remembers the way she and Jack walked arm in arm to the Toyota. It is as if she can still see, down to the last detail, the way the steam rose off the bitumen in puffs of smoke. The beach was narrow, in a valley between two high headlands; it was the whole world. Jack lit a Winfield and they looked back. The hailstones. They are melting away, returning the beach to itself, but leaving a million pockmarks in the sand.

ACKNOWLEDGEMENTS

THE AUTHOR WOULD LIKE to acknowledge the financial support of the Ontario Arts Council and the Toronto Arts Council.

Some of these stories appeared in earlier versions and under different titles in the following literary magazines and journals: *Antipodes: A North American Journal of Australian Literature*; *B&A*; *Descant*; *Qwerty*; *Taddle Creek*; and *White Wall Review*. My thanks go to those editors for their support.

Note on "Lyrebird" — although this story is fiction, it is loosely inspired by a real event. In 1816 there was a massacre of the Dharawal people at Broughton Pass, Appin, in western Sydney, in which, among other killings, aboriginal women and children were driven over a cliff. The massacre at Appin differed from subsequent massacres in that British troops, rather than police or private citizens, initiated it (Professional Historians Association Inc., NSW, "Broughton Pass Aboriginal Massacre Site," in Register of Historic Places and Objects, SRI Number 4671006, 2001).

I am indebted to Philip Drew's book *The Coast Dwellers* for his profound discussion on Australian life as it has evolved, and is lived, on the coast.

Thanks go to my agent, Dean Cooke, my editor at Raincoast, Lynn Henry, and the friends over the years who read and helped these stories along the way.

Finally, as always, my love and gratitude to my first reader, Wendy Morgan.